SHE'LL BE COMING DOWN
THE MOUNTAIN . . .

" . . . I'll put Eli up in the sheriff's jail, wait for the first train south, then we'll be on our way to Denver," Longarm said.

"I see," Miss Noble said. "And if—"

She never finished her sentence for, in the next moment, their coach lurched violently to the side and lifted. Longarm grabbed the arm of his seat as the entire train tilted. The sound of Miss Noble screaming did not drown out the explosion somewhere up ahead. Was it an avalanche?

Longarm reached out to grab Miss Noble, but then he was flying too as the coach began to tumble down the mountainside. He lost consciousness as the sound of tearing metal and splintering wood filled his ears like the roar of a killer Kansas tornado . . .

DON'T MISS THESE
ALL-ACTION WESTERN SERIES
FROM THE BERKLEY PUBLISHING GROUP

THE GUNSMITH by J. R. Roberts

Clint Adams was a legend among lawmen, outlaws, and ladies. They called him . . . the Gunsmith.

LONGARM by Tabor Evans

The popular long-running series about U.S. Deputy Marshal Long—his life, his loves, his fight for justice.

LONE STAR by Wesley Ellis

The blazing adventures of Jessica Starbuck and the martial arts master, Ki. Over eight million copies in print.

SLOCUM by Jake Logan

Today's longest-running action Western. John Slocum rides a deadly trail of hot blood and cold steel.

TABOR EVANS

LONGARM

AND THE TRAIN ROBBERS

JOVE BOOKS, NEW YORK

LONGARM AND THE TRAIN ROBBERS

A Jove Book / published by arrangement with
the author

PRINTING HISTORY
Jove edition / February 1994

ISBN: 0-515-11313-1

A JOVE BOOK®
Jove Books are published by The Berkley Publishing Group,
200 Madison Avenue, New York, New York 10016.
JOVE and the "J" design are trademarks belonging
to Jove Publications, Inc.

PRINTED IN THE UNITED STATES OF AMERICA

10 9 8 7 6 5 4 3 2 1

Chapter 1

Deputy Custis Long stared past his manacled prisoner through the Union Pacific train's window and saw a pair of elk hurrying down from the western slopes of the Laramie Mountains to escape an advancing snowstorm. He looked up at the lead-gray underbelly of an ocean of deep, rumbling clouds, and could feel their Union Pacific railroad car being buffeted by the icy northern winds.

"We're going to get a real sonofabitch of a storm," Eli Wheat said, fogging up the window with his hot, fetid breath. "I'd guess that we might not even make it over the Laramie Mountains. Be a damned shame, wouldn't it, Deputy?"

"Yeah," Longarm said drily. "A real shame. Might mean that we'd have to delay your necktie party a few extra days."

"I sure wouldn't bitch about that," Eli said, his dark features shaping into a twisted grin. "Might be that I could even find a way to delay things a bit longer than expected."

1

"You try it," Longarm said, "and all you'll get for your trouble is another good pistol-whipping."

"You like to use that gun barrel of yours to part a man's hair, don't you?" Eli challenged, his voice turning nasty.

"Just shut up," Longarm snapped.

But Eli wouldn't shut up. He could see the snowstorm moving down from the Laramie Mountains, and that their train was charging right into its face. He could feel the train losing speed as it began the steep ascent into the rugged mountains, and every second that the mountains and the storm delayed the train was to his advantage.

"Could be," Eli said, voice growing loud so that all the passengers could hear, "that this is a real blizzard that we're facing. Could be that we might *derail* or something up there and all of us freeze to death."

Longarm noticed several of the other passengers pale. A pretty, auburn-haired young woman in her twenties just a few seats up shot a glance back over her shoulder, and Longarm could see that she was upset. It was growing colder in their car, and Longarm made a mental note to upbraid their conductor for not keeping the coach's wood-burning stove hot.

"Yes, sir!" Eli Wheat crowed. "I guess if I got to die, I'd sure rather it be by freezin' than having to dance at the end of a rope while a crowd of—"

Longarm reached across his body with his left hand and clamped it on Eli's throat, cutting off the man's words. His powerful fingers bit into Eli's windpipe, and he held his grip like a steel trap while Eli tried to smile and show that he was tough. A full minute passed and the killer's face grew bright red. His eyes bugged and he began to make gagging sounds.

2

"Let him go!" the young woman demanded, jumping from her seat. "You can't choke him to death like that!"

Longarm released his grip. Eli began to choke and suck for air. He was trembling and gagging and having an awful time. Other passengers, no longer able to ignore the disturbing sounds, turned, and their eyes said that they too did not approve of Longarm's method of silencing his prisoner.

"You ought to be ashamed of yourself!" the pretty young woman scolded, coming to stand beside Longarm. She was shaking with fury. "What kind of a monster are you anyway? That man must be terrified."

"Terrified?" Longarm took a moment to curb his own anger. "Miss . . ."

"Noble. Martha Noble."

"Well, Miss Noble," Longarm said, "I can see that you are a sympathetic young woman. One possessing high-minded purpose and ideals."

"I wouldn't choke another human being just to prove how big and strong I am," Miss Noble said. "I wouldn't do what you just did to that poor man any more than I'd choke a kitten or a puppy."

Longarm heard several of the other passengers muttering in agreement. Eli was still choking and coughing, but it sounded forced to Longarm.

"This man is no kitten or puppy, Miss Noble," Longarm said, trying to explain, although he thought no explanation was due or even deserved. "Eli Wheat is a cold-blooded killer of men, women, and even children."

Miss Noble took a step back. She blinked and looked at Eli in disbelief. He made an attempt to smile. There were tears in his eyes and he looked beaten and submissive.

3

Miss Noble said, "I . . . I doubt that."

"Why?" Longarm asked. "Because he looks harmless? Of course he does! He's handcuffed and wearing leg manacles. But the man is a notorious stage and train robber. Eli, how many trains have you and your gang robbed?"

"Not a single one!"

Longarm snorted with derision. "That's a bald-faced lie. Eli and his friends have robbed at least four that we know of, and probably many more. They've derailed trains and ambushed dozens of stagecoaches. Their favorite method is just to shoot the driver, the guard, and a lead horse all in one volley. Needless to say, the safety of passengers concerns them not a whit."

Miss Noble started to say something, but Longarm wasn't finished educating her. "Less than a week ago, Eli broke into a sod house and murdered an entire family. A good wife, a fine husband, and their two sons."

"I find that impossible to believe!"

"I didn't do it!" Eli choked. "The deputy is just sayin' that so's he can mistreat me!"

Longarm ached to drive his right elbow into Eli's solar plexus hard enough to shut him up for a good long time. The memory of finding that family of murdered sodbusters was going to haunt him for a good long while.

"How long has it been since your prisoner has had anything to eat?" Miss Noble demanded.

Longarm ignored the question. His eyes took in the other accusing faces. "Listen," he said, "I know Eli isn't particularly mean-looking, but neither is a wolf if you happen to catch sight of one playing with its pups."

4

Eli started to say something, but Longarm cut him off with a withering glance.

Miss Noble went back to her seat, and on the way said loudly, "We wouldn't stand to watch an animal chained and mistreated that way, and yet we allow one human being to do it to another."

Longarm ground his teeth in anger and frustration. He'd met too damn many women like Miss Noble. They were well-intentioned but incredibly naive. He'd bet Miss Noble would also be opposed to demon whiskey and up to her pretty eyebrows in religion. Undoubtedly, she could quote the Bible for hours and was the product of a very sheltered existence. She'd never have seen another human being murdered, and she would find it in her heart to forgive any sin believing that was what God expected.

Longarm hoped that Miss Noble never saw the real savagery that a man like Eli Wheat was capable of exhibiting. One minute Eli could be whining and slightly pathetic-looking; the next he could turn more vicious and deadlier than a cornered Apache.

Longarm stared out the window. The first flakes of snow were beginning to swirl in the air. The train was rapidly slowing, and Longarm could see that the wall of flying snow was less than a thousand yards up the mountain.

"It looks bad," Eli said, his voice a tortured whisper. "Real bad."

"It's nothing for this train. Hell, the tracks are clear and even if it is snowing hard up on the summit, the storm is just arriving so the snow can't be very deep. We'll get through without much delay, you can bet on that."

5

Eli loudly cleared his bruised throat. "If I had any money, I'd bet against us reaching Cheyenne in time to catch that southbound train into Denver. That's what I'd bet."

Longarm stood up and stepped into the aisle. Although he had stretched and walked up and down the aisle several times when they had been taking on coal and water in Laramie, he already felt stiff and restless. He was a big man who wore a brown tweed suit, a blue-gray shirt with a shoestring tie, and comfortably low-heeled army boots of cordovan leather. His brown Stetson was flat-crowned and somewhat the worse for wear, but his clothes were clean. A gold chain connected an Ingersoll watch in one vest pocket to a twin-barreled, .44-caliber derringer in the other.

"Excuse me," he said as another passenger squeezed past him in the aisle and they bumped because of the rolling motion of the coach. "It's a little cramped in those seats."

"Maybe you should also let your prisoner stretch," Miss Noble snipped.

Longarm ignored the woman's suggestion. Always suspicious that a prisoner might have friends waiting for an unguarded moment to act, he surveyed the coach, eyes skipping over every single passenger. None seemed to be the type that would pose a danger. Unfortunately, this train was packed, every seat filled. And although the wind was finding cracks to seep into the car and cause it to become decidedly chilly, there were so many bodies crammed into the coach that the air was stuffy.

"We're really starting to climb now," Eli said. "I don't think this old train is going to make it over the summit in this storm."

"It'll make it," Longarm said, knowing that it would be a slow and difficult pull over the 8,600-foot Laramie Summit. If the snow was really heavy, they might even be forced to attack it with snow shovels or plows.

"Even if we do, it'll still be the longest sixty miles you ever rode," Eli predicted. "Sixty miles doesn't seem like much, but a lot can happen."

"Shut up," Longarm growled, dropping back into his seat, "or I'll part your hair permanently."

Eli smiled, but there was no warmth in it. He was a hatchet-faced man, lean and muscular. Dressed in a heavy woolen jacket and baggy pants, and slumped down next to the window, he looked deceptively mild and even vulnerable.

Longarm knew better. Eli was a dead-eye shot. He probably stood about five feet ten and weighed less than 170 pounds, but every pound was bone and muscle, and he was as quick with a gun as any man that Longarm had ever crossed. Facing a gallows in Denver made him capable of any act of murder and desperation.

Miss Noble climbed to her feet. Shooting a look of pure venom at Longarm, she squared her shoulders and rummaged around in a brown paper sack. After a moment, she extracted an apple and a sandwich wrapped in crisp brown paper. Longarm knew at once that it was not a peace offering.

"Deputy," Miss Noble said, "perhaps I was a little harsh in my criticism of you. That doesn't mean that, for even a minute, I believe this man is capable of the heinous acts you say he committed, but—"

"He shot the sodbuster in the face with his own scattergun," Longarm said in a clipped, uncompromising

7

voice. "Then my prisoner used that same scattergun to brain the oldest son, who was about eighteen."

"Stop it!" Miss Noble cried, shrinking away in horror.

But Longarm was angry. This woman hadn't been invited to interfere, and she needed to have a lesson in reality so that the next time she saw a lawman and his prisoner, she might be a fairer judge of who deserved her acid tongue.

"After he killed the father and oldest son," Longarm continued, "my prisoner went into the house and when the fifteen-year-old son attacked him, my prisoner used his knife. It wasn't much of a fight because Mr. Wheat is very, very good with a bowie. The boy had no chance at all."

Miss Noble paled. The sandwich tumbled from her grip, and Eli reached out and snatched it up. He stuffed it whole into his mouth and began to engulf it like a snake swallowing a big gopher.

"I'm not going to tell you the details about how this prisoner killed the wife and mother," Longarm said, taking pity on Miss Noble. "But I will tell you this much— it wasn't pretty and it wasn't a quick, merciful death. And so you see, I don't care if this man hangs or I have the pleasure of killing him before we reach Denver."

Miss Noble swayed as a sudden and powerful gust of wind rocked their coach. She appeared faint, and could not seem to tear her eyes off Eli as he licked his thin lips.

"Miss Noble, you look unwell. Why don't you take a seat?" Longarm said, feeling a little guilty because he had been so forthright in his account of the murder.

8

Another passenger who had also been glaring at Longarm now turned his icy gaze on Eli, who seemed oblivious to everything.

"Deputy, how did you ever manage to capture that . . . that monster?"

"He made the mistake of stealing the sodbuster's horses and cutting southwest toward Utah. Eli didn't realize that country is damned rocky and neither of the sodbuster's horses were shod. They went lame up in the Unita Mountains, and I was able to overtake Eli and catch him asleep right at dawn."

Eli's face turned bitter. "Damned sonsabitchin' plow horses!"

The other man introduced himself. "My name is Edward Ashmore and I'm the president of the Bank of Wyoming with headquarters in Cheyenne. We're opening a second branch in Laramie and I'm constantly traveling back and forth between those places. Fifty miles doesn't seem like a long journey by rail, except that it's all up and then down a mountain. It's a tedious and even dangerous roadbed."

"I know that," Longarm said. "There are a lot of switchbacks, and I've been over this stretch in winter when the trains had a terrible time crossing."

"I'm hoping that, it only being November, we won't get the kind of snowstorm we might get a month or two from now."

"I hope you're right," Longarm said, looking out the window and seeing that the snow was thick now and visibility was just forty or fifty yards.

"I for one," Ashmore said, "understand that there are such men as your prisoner. I've never witnessed a killing or been to war. But I've lived in Wyoming more than ten years now and I know that there are desperate and ruthless outlaws. Men perfectly capable of murder. Deputy Long, you're to be congratulated for taking every precaution against allowing this man to escape and attempt to murder one of us."

"I appreciate your support," Longarm said, loud enough so that Miss Noble could not possibly fail to hear. "A lawman never seems to get much respect, and we damn sure don't get much pay either. But someone has to track down fugitives of the law and bring them to justice."

"Tell me, have you ever considered some other occupation?"

"Such as?"

The banker shrugged. "The Bank of Wyoming could use an ex-lawman to guard shipments between Cheyenne and Laramie. I like your no-nonsense style. You strike me as a true professional, sir."

Longarm warmed to the praise. "I sincerely appreciate your kind and flattering words. But the fact of the matter is that I like my work. Oh, I grumble about the hours and the bad pay. I sometimes even envy a sheriff or town marshal who can go home to a wife and children. I'm constantly being sent hither and yon after escaped fugitives. But I'm good at it, and in fact I think there are few better."

The banker smiled. "Yes, yes, I'm sure that's true. You're exactly the kind of a man that we could use to protect our interests. There's a bright future in Wyoming banking for a steady man who can handle himself. I'm sure that we could offer you a salary that would make you give up that badge."

"Thanks, but I'm just not interested."

Ashmore looked genuinely surprised. "I'm not used to being turned down when I offer a man an exceptionally well-paying job. Is there . . . is there something personal you have against me, sir?"

"Oh, no! I just like my work and right now I'm trying to keep my mind on my prisoner. Maybe the next time I come through Cheyenne I can look you up and we can talk."

"By then the position might be filled."

"That's a chance I'll just have to take," Longarm said, trying but failing to sound concerned because he doubted that he'd have any real interest in being a bank guard no matter how good the pay.

"I'm going to raise hell with our conductor for letting this coach get so frigid," the banker said, rubbing his hands briskly together. "It's outrageous!"

Longarm glanced around. "I haven't seen him for quite some time."

"I'll go look for him," the banker said, loud enough for everyone to hear. "I'm not about to let these good people, many of whom are undoubtedly faithful depositors at the Bank of Wyoming, suffer because of a dereliction of duty."

"Good idea," Longarm said, noting how the storm and the train had finally met so that visibility outside was reduced to nothing.

Eli stared at the window, the muscles of his jaw distended. In a quiet voice he said, "I'm not going to hang."

"That's not my business," Longarm said. "All I'm sworn to do is bring you to trial."

"Yeah, but you don't know what happened back there at that homestead."

11

Longarm's voice dropped to a hard whisper. "Oh, yes I do! I can read signs and I know you slaughtered that entire family."

"They weren't neighborly to me," Eli said between clenched teeth. "The sodbuster, he wouldn't give me a fair trade for two lame horses. All I wanted was a fair trade!"

"So you blew his face off? Tell it to the judge after I tell him about the wife and the sons."

"They were mean to me!" Eli hissed. "Didn't even ask me in for supper after I said I was hungry."

"That's no reason to kill them."

"They *asked* for it!"

"Shut up," Longarm breathed. "If I wasn't a deputy of the federal court in Denver, I'd have gut-shot you up in the Unitas and been done with it. You deserve to die hard, Eli. A bullet in your brain would be too kind."

Eli glanced sideways at Longarm. "You're no different than me," he said. "You just hide behind a badge so you can do your killing legal."

Longarm's eyes shifted to the man, then past him to the window. Even over the pounding of the iron wheels he could hear the sound of the wind howling off the Laramie Mountains. This storm was coming all the way down from Canada. Longarm could only imagine what kind of a white, frozen hell the locomotive engineer must be fighting as he peered vainly ahead into the freezing maelstrom, trying to gauge where each of the many switchbacks would be and hoping that the snow did not stick on the ground to block the rails.

"I never liked snow until now," Eli said with a smirk. "I always said that I was going to California. That's where

12

I was headed when you caught me. I'd never have killed again."

"That's a lie. You've killed so often that it means nothing to you anymore. That woman whose throat you cut in Denver was—"

"Was just another tired-out old whore!" Eli choked out. "She tried to get me drunk so that her boyfriend could steal the money from my pants. But I was wise to 'em! If he hadn't jumped out of that hotel window, I'd have killed him too."

Longarm didn't know if Miss Martha Noble had over-heard this confession, but he suspected that she had and was probably starting to realize that she'd made a fool of herself defending such a cold-blooded killer.

A few minutes later, the conductor and the banker returned. The banker looked angry and the conductor began to pitch wood into the small stove at the rear of the car.

"I'd never hire him," the banker said loudly. "A man like that wouldn't last a day at our Bank of Wyoming but he'll last forever on this railroad. I tell you, the Union Pacific will hire anyone!"

Longarm smiled to himself. The banker was putting on a show of authority for the other passengers and was making sure that everyone knew about his bank. Loud, boastful people were irritating to Longarm, who preferred to go about his work with a quiet efficiency. He never bragged or told stories of the men he tracked down and brought to justice.

Longarm and other passengers seemed to hold their breath as the train inched its way up the summit. Time lost all meaning. It was as if they were traveling in a tunnel of ice. There was nothing to see outside and the storm kept screeching like a tormented witch. But finally, the train seemed to level out and pause, then slightly pick-up speed.

"We've done it," Longarm declared loudly. "We've crested the summit!"

"Are you sure?" Miss Noble asked.

"He's right," the banker said, beaming. "I've been over this stretch a hundred times. There is no question about it. We've crested and are now on the downhill run."

"But isn't that just as dangerous?" another passenger asked. "I mean, what if we were to lose our brakes?"

"There is no chance of that," an older man wearing bib overalls and work boots declared. "I worked on a railroad for twenty years back in Ohio. Our brakes aren't going to fail."

Everyone except Eli Wheat seemed much relieved. Studying his wedge-shaped face with his hooked nose and deep-set eyes, Longarm said, "Looks like we're going to make Cheyenne after all. Another two hours at the most."

Eli turned and stared right through him. "Don't bet your life on it, Deputy."

"What is that supposed to mean?"

Eli smiled. "It means that a lot can happen in two hours and this blizzard is getting worse, not better."

Longarm stared at the whipping snow curtain. He could hear the intensity of the storm grow and he knew that Eli was right. The ride down from this high summit was risky even under the best of circumstances, and these were the worst of circumstances.

Miss Noble turned around and favored Longarm with what he judged to be an embarrassed smile.

14

"I . . . I couldn't help but overhear your conversation about those two people that your prisoner attacked in Denver."

"Then you know that he killed the woman."

"Yes," she said in a sad voice. "I heard that. And I guess that I do owe you an apology."

"Apology accepted," Longarm said. "And I probably shouldn't have grabbed Eli by the throat and tried to throttle him into silence."

"Damn right you shouldn't have!" Eli spat out.

"Shut up," Longarm ordered.

Martha Noble sighed. "I will be oh so glad when we reach Cheyenne."

"I suppose that you have family waiting for you there?"

"No. I'm not married. I was once but, well . . . it didn't work out."

"I'm sorry."

"I'm not. My husband was not a nice man. He wasn't a murderer or anything, but he had no character."

Longarm nodded as if to say he understood.

"Marshal, will you be staying long in Cheyenne?"

"Only as long as necessary. I'll put Eli up in the sheriff's jail, wait for the first train south, then we'll be on our way to Denver."

"I see," Miss Noble said. "And if—"

Martha Noble never finished her sentence for, in the next moment, their coach lurched violently to the side and lifted. Martha screamed and Longarm grabbed the arm of his seat as the entire train tilted.

Eli raised his handcuffs and tried to claw out Longarm's eyes. But the coach tottered and before Eli could reach Longarm, it began a sickening roll.

The sound of Miss Noble screaming in Longarm's face did not drown out an explosion somewhere up ahead. Was it perhaps an avalanche?

Longarm reached to grab Miss Noble as she left her feet, but then he was flying too as the coach began to tumble down the mountainside. He lost consciousness as the sound of tearing metal and splintering wood filled his ears like a roar of a killer Kansas tornado.

Chapter 2

Longarm awoke slowly to the moan of the icy mountain wind and the anguished cries and pleas for help of the surviving passengers. He was aware of movement within the overturned coach, and when he tried to raise himself to his hands and knees, a shooting pain radiated across the back of his head.

He gritted his teeth, fighting to remain conscious. Light was almost nonexistent inside the coach, and Longarm could not distinguish anything. Close beside him a woman groaned and then cried softly. Longarm reached out to comfort her.

"Ma'am," he whispered, suddenly aware of the intense cold and blowing snow. "Ma'am, it's going to be all right. There will be help on the way."

"Why is it so dark?"

Longarm recognized Miss Noble's voice. "Maybe we're covered by snow. Maybe it's just the blizzard blocking out the sun. I can't say for sure until I get out and look around."

"Where is your prisoner?"

17

"I don't know, Miss Noble. But I'll find out soon enough."

With his right hand, Longarm reached up and felt a deep laceration in his scalp. No wonder he felt drugged and could hardly think straight. Longarm reached into his pocket and dug for a match. He used his thumbnail to scratch the match into life, and when he raised it up to survey the carnage and destruction, Longarm was appalled to see so many dead and injured.

There was blood everywhere, and most of the windows of the overturned coach were shattered, allowing the blizzard its deadly entry. Already, some of the bodies were covered with a white shroud of snow. The coach was lying on its side, but badly canted downward. Longarm was sure that their coach would have rolled even farther had it not been caught by an obstruction poking out of the steep mountainside. A sudden gust of wind extinguished Longarm's match and plunged the scene back into darkness.

Longarm lit another match, shielding its flickering light from the hard, blowing wind. He took a longer second look, specifically searching for his prisoner. Eli Wheat was gone. Longarm was sure of it. He was also sure that the approach of night would soon drive the freezing temperatures to a killing low and that, if he did not take measures to save not only himself but the other passengers, they'd all be frozen solid before morning.

"Deputy Long, we've got to help these people!"

Longarm turned and held the dying match up toward Miss Noble. She had been cut up a little by flying glass and appeared badly shaken.

Longarm's match burned out, and he squeezed the woman's arm in a feeble attempt to reassure her that all would be fine. "Miss Noble, it's a wonder that our stove didn't ignite and turn this coach into a funeral pyre. The stove must have been thrown outside and then extinguished."

"I don't know. But it's freezing in here."

"I need some light," Longarm told her. "We have to find a lantern or we'll never be able to help the injured."

"I think a lot of them are dead!" the young woman exclaimed, her voice near the breaking point.

"But we can't worry about that. We have to do what we can for those that can still be saved. Can you move around, Miss Noble? Are your legs . . ."

"They're fine."

Longarm heard her take a deep, steadying breath. He was encouraged when she said, "What can I do to help?"

"Let's get outside and see what happened to the rest of the train. Perhaps there are other coaches that fared better and that will offer shelter."

"It's a miracle that any of us are alive."

"We need a doctor," Longarm said.

"That would be a second miracle."

Taking the woman's hand and forcing himself to ignore the pleading of injured and confused passengers, Longarm struggled out through a window. The blizzard attacked him with demented vengence. The snow sheeted in horizontally, and visibility was less than ten feet.

"I can't see anything!" Miss Noble cried.

"Me neither," Longarm said, hanging onto the woman's hand. "But we must find out if anyone else survived. We *must* find help!"

Lowering their heads, Longarm and the woman struggled forward along the overturned train. They passed another coach which had broken apart and was ominously silent. Then a third coach loomed up and Longarm saw what he believed to be a glow of light from its interior. This coach had come to rest in an almost upright position.

"Stay with me!" he hollered into the storm as he fought his way to the rear door of the coach. Doubling up his fists, he pounded on the door over and over until it opened a crack.

"Let us in!" he bellowed.

The door crashed open. Strong hands grabbed Longarm and Miss Noble and hauled them inside. A moment later, the door was jammed shut and Longarm had to wipe ice from his eyelashes in order to see. The survivors of this coach had righted their stove, but not before it had consumed an entire row of seats. Now, they were feeding the life-giving fire scraps from other chairs and trying to close the broken windows with seat cushions and blankets.

Longarm had the impression of being in a cluttered cave. He guessed there were two dozen passengers. Some were in bad shape, but most eyed him with astonishment.

"Who are you?" a man finally asked, breaking the silence.

"I'm Deputy U.S. Marshal Custis Long. Is anyone here in charge?"

No one stepped forward, but one man did say, "We lost about eight and two among us have internal injuries. We could sure use a doctor."

"I know that. Has anyone gone in search of other survivors? This might be the only real shelter."

"I went up toward the front of the train, but all the coaches were destroyed," a big man in a heavy sheepskin-lined coat answered. "And the locomotive wasn't any-where around. It must have rolled all the way down the mountain."

"Miss Noble and I crawled out of a coach two cars back," Longarm said. "The next one back is demolished. I doubt that anyone survived. *Our* coach has at least twenty people trapped inside. I need able-bodied volunteers to bring them here."

"Why, here!" a man bellowed in anger. "This is *our* coach. Why don't they—"

"We need to stay bunched and close together, that's why!" Longarm said angrily. "This coach is still in one piece and you've got a fire. If we can pack a hundred people in here, they'll all likely survive this storm."

"But . . ."

"What is wrong with you?" Miss Noble cried, stepping in front of Longarm and confronting the man. "There are other people back there dying! Have you no charity in your heart?"

The man tried to match her eyes, but then broke away and turned to the fire.

"Like I said," Longarm repeated, "I need volunteers. If we don't get all the injured into this coach, they'll die of exposure."

"I'm coming," the man who had protested said, whirling around and starting for the door.

"Zeke," a woman said to him, "you take my coat while you're out in that storm. And don't you fall off this mountain."

"I won't, Liz. I swear I won't," Zeke promised as he took his wife's coat.

"I want to come too," Martha Noble said. "I met some

wonderful people in that coach. I'm not about to stay here while their lives are in danger."

"All right," Longarm said, proud of the young woman.

Other passengers, perhaps shamed by Martha's courage, were soon following Longarm back out into the storm. The wind was blowing so hard that it knocked them down when they passed the open areas between the overturned cars and were exposed to its full, unopposed force. Three of the rescuers were not strong enough to stand up to the fierce gusts and had to crawl back to safety, but the others, with Longarm in front, struggled on until they arrived at the coach.

"It'll be dark soon!" he yelled, knowing that his words could not be heard by most of the rescuers. "We have to get the survivors to shelter now!"

Longarm had to fight through a blanket of snow in order to crawl back inside. Once inside, he tried to get a match, but his unprotected hands were numb and useless. With no alternative, Longarm began to grope around in the coach for anyone who moved. One delirious passenger screamed and clawed at Longarm's face, but he easily subdued the frightened woman.

"Calm down, ma'am. It's all right!" he yelled. "We're getting you out of here!"

She gradually came to understand. Moments later, the woman was eased out into the storm and Longarm was moving on to another victim. And so it went until time lost all meaning. Longarm did not know how many people he roused and helped guide out of the coach, but it had to be several dozen.

The dead bodies he found were so stiff Longarm reckoned that they were already beginning to freeze solid. He had to work in darkness, so there was no way of recognizing faces. All that Longarm knew for sure was that, every time he guided a survivor back to Martha Noble or one of the others, he was definitely saving a life.

Exhausted, frozen, and working in total darkness, Longarm stayed until he was absolutely certain that there were no other survivors. The last few people that he helped to remove were undoubtedly in critical shape and barely able to respond to his urgings. Not once did Longarm touch a person or a body that wore handcuffs and manacles. Eli Wheat was gone. Longarm couldn't explain how or where the killer could have gone to, but there was little doubt that the man had somehow escaped.

"What about the other coaches?" Martha asked after they had finally returned to warmth and shelter two coaches forward.

"I don't know," Longarm said, listening to the shrieking wind. "You heard what the man said."

Martha pressed close. "Do you think he could have been mistaken?"

Longarm's head was throbbing and he was so cold and drained that he had begun to shiver despite the fact that the interior of the coach was packed with humanity and the temperature was slightly above freezing.

"Your coat is too light," Martha said. "You must use mine."

"I couldn't fit into it even if I wanted to, which I don't," Longarm said, teeth chattering like dice in a cup.

Martha touched Longarm's face; then her hand dropped to unbutton his light coat. She pushed him down and unbuttoned her own coat, then pulled it close around them. Longarm felt the instant warmth of her body. He wrapped his arms around her and held the woman tight.

"You were magnificent today," Martha breathed into his ear. "If you hadn't demanded that the able-bodied in this coach join us, we couldn't possibly have saved so many lives."

"You were pretty great yourself," he replied. "I owe you an apology for the mean-spirited things I was thinking about you before."

"Because of that prisoner?"

"Yes. Eli Wheat really is a vicious murderer."

"I know that now. I guess I even knew it then. I should never have interfered. I don't even know what possessed me to—"

"Dear repentant woman," Longarm said interrupting, "has anyone ever said that you talk a lot?"

"It's been mentioned," Martha said with a smile. "I get that from my father. He was an attorney, and I plan to also practice law when we reach Cheyenne. It's a new challenge for me, but I know the law far better than most men who hang out their shingle."

"I've never seen a woman lawyer before, but I'm sure that you'll do fine," Longarm said. "There's probably plenty of women that would rather deal with another woman."

"There's even more men that would rather deal with a woman," she told him.

Longarm was sure that was true. Martha Noble was very attractive, and he'd rather deal with her anytime than another man.

"Custis? That is your name, isn't it?"

"Yes."

"Well, Custis, I still say that you were acting beyond your authority when you almost throttled that prisoner."

"I wish now that I had. But if I manage to recapture Eli Wheat, you can defend him in court if you choose."

When the woman offered no comment, Longarm chuckled. "So, I'm holding a pretty attorney in a very compromising position. Martha, are you going to sue me for damages if I try to steal a kiss?"

"You can kiss me all you want," she whispered. "I've never been kissed by a hero before. So kiss me."

Longarm did kiss Miss Noble. He kissed her until his teeth no longer chattered and his passion momentarily swept away the nightmare of the train wreck. And then, he kissed her a little more.

"I wish we were somewhere else," he confessed, squeezing her. "Somewhere nice and warm in Cheyenne."

"What do you think happened?"

"You mean to the train, or to my prisoner?"

"Both."

Longarm closed his eyes. "I thought, just for an instant before we went over the mountainside, that I heard an explosion."

"You mean like dynamite?"

"Exactly. It could have been an avalanche or a boulder that broke loose up above and came crashing down to derail the entire train, but I doubt it. We won't know for sure until help arrives and this blizzard passes."

"Do you believe that it might have had something to do with your prisoner?"

"Maybe."

"But wouldn't the risk of killing him have been too great?"

"Eli had everything to gain and nothing to lose," Longarm said. "If you'll remember, I told you that he belonged to a gang of cutthroats that robbed stagecoaches and trains. They've derailed the Union Pacific before with dynamite. Sometimes pitching it under the moving train, sometimes just blowing up track in front of the locomotive."

Martha Noble choked with rage. "So, in order to give one ruthless and convicted murderer a slim chance to escape, this gang was willing to sacrifice dozens of innocent passengers and train employees."

"That's the size of it. If it was the same gang that Eli belonged to, they will have broken into the mail car and dynamited the safe in order to steal whatever cash and valuables it might have contained."

"And executed any guards that might have survived," Martha said bitterly.

"Of course."

"What a fool I was to upbraid you earlier today!"

"Don't let it bother you for a minute," Longarm told the young attorney. "Just . . . well, just chalk this up to experience. Eli has that hangdog look that makes everyone think he's a victim rather than the victimizer. I think that's why the man is so dangerous."

Martha was silent a long time. "I hope to God that there are other train coaches like this that people have managed to reach. That one destroyed coach we passed looked like a pile of chopped firewood. I can't imagine what—"

"Don't think about it," Longarm said. "That doesn't help. We have to just worry about saving ourselves now. We have to hope that, when this train didn't arrive in Cheyenne, help was dispatched right away."

"In a storm like this?" Martha looked up at him in the dim glow of the firelight. "I doubt that they would send anyone out in this weather. Would you?"

"No," Longarm admitted. "I'd wait until the worst of this storm passed."

Martha thought about that for a few minutes before she said, "If some of these people don't get to a doctor soon, they'll die."

Longarm knew that. He also knew that it was pointless to worry about what was beyond their control. Each and every passenger had been attended to as well as possible given the extreme deprivations they were all trying to endure and survive.

"Wyoming storms this early in the year often pass quickly," Longarm said. "I think those among us that survive until morning will crawl out into sunlight."

"I want to believe that," Martha whispered as she held Longarm and her body heat drove away his chills.

When Longarm awoke, he knew that his greatest wish had been granted. The wind had stopped and, looking outside through a window that was still intact, he could see the morning sun melting the snow. Longarm kissed Martha awake, and then he joined those who were able to crawl out into the brilliant sunlight. For a few moments, they were all a little dazed and confused, like wild animals emerging from hibernation.

The train was segmented like a broken logger's chain, pieces of it scattered all up and down the mountainside. The locomotive had tumbled hundreds of feet farther down into the gorge, and lay with its huge driving wheels reaching for the sky. The coal car was nearby. Another coach now

27

rested several hundred yards above both and was wrapped around an immense pine tree.

It took only a few minutes for Longarm to realize that there were no other survivors from the train. Every coach except two had been ripped apart, with bodies and baggage now buried under a thick blanket of glistening snowfall.

"Where are you going?" Martha asked.

"To the mail car, or what's left of it."

Martha followed Longarm about fifty yards up the slope. The mail car was a pile of kindling, and it took Longarm several minutes to dig his way through the rubble in order to reach what had been a large safe. The safe would have survived the destruction had it not been dynamited. Now its massive door hung from only one hinge. The safe itself had been emptied. Even the mail sacks had been rifled and their contents scattered everywhere.

"The safe was dynamited," Longarm announced when he crawled back out and rejoined Martha.

She stared at him, struck by the implications of his words. "Then this whole thing was a deliberate act by Eli Wheat's gang."

"It could have been another bunch. Eli's friends don't have a corner on train robberies. Still, I think that they probably wanted to see if they could free one of their own and at the same time make a good haul."

"So what now?"

Longarm looked up at the sky, and then removed and studied his pocket watch. "It's only eight-fifteen," he said, repocketing the Ingersoll. "My guess is that a rescue party ought to be here before nine o'clock."

"With a doctor?"

28

"I would think so," Longarm said. "The Union Pacific officials might believe that this train just mired down in a snowbank, but they'll know that there will be passengers who are suffering from the cold and possibly even frostbite. I'm sure that they'll bring along at least one doctor."

"When we reach Cheyenne, what will you do?" Martha asked.

Longarm turned to survey the destruction below. How many frozen bodies were buried in those coaches and lying hidden by the white death?

"I'll telegraph Denver and report what happened and my findings. Then I'll go after Eli and his gang."

"By yourself?"

"Yes," Longarm said. "But even if I fail, there will be plenty of others hunting that gang. Even Pinkertons. But I mean to find them first and have the pleasure of killing or capturing Eli and his friends. I want them very bad, Martha. And though you might disapprove, I'll smile when they prance like puppets at the end of a hangman's noose."

"I don't disapprove," she said. "In fact, I rather hope you'll send me an invitation to that party."

Longarm had not realized the depth of change that this young woman had undergone in less than twenty-four hours. No longer was she blind to the evil that lurked in men like Eli Wheat. It was, on the one hand, sad to see her lose her innocence. But on the other hand, if Martha Noble hoped to survive as a rare female Wyoming attorney, she was long overdue for a massive dose of frontier reality.

Chapter 3

True to Longarm's prediction, a relief and supply train with a massive snowplow mounted to its locomotive's cowcatcher came puffing up from Cheyenne at about nine o'clock. No doubt those arriving had expected to find a train stranded in deep drifts. Whatever their expectations, they could not have anticipated the devastation that lay scattered across the mountainside.

Longarm and Martha, standing side by side and arm in arm, witnessed their shock. Longarm saw the Union Pacific's relief road crew gape at the carnage and then slowly step off the rescue train and plod forward.

"What in God's name happened?" a tall man in a green flannel shirt cried, yanking off his railroad cap and wringing it in his big fists. "Dear Lord, the telegraph lines between Cheyenne and Laramie went down yesterday afternoon. We just figured that maybe this train had returned to Laramie."

"Obviously not," Longarm said as more men came up. "Did you bring a doctor?"

"Why, no!"

"You should have," Longarm said quickly. "We've got some badly injured passengers and more dead ones than I care to think about."

"But what . . ."

"It was sabotage," Longarm said, flashing his federal badge. "Dynamite. They struck the line during the blizzard and we were all over the mountainside before we knew what hit us. I'm afraid that the death toll is very high."

"What about Art Becker, the locomotive engineer? And Scotty Macintosh, the fireman?"

Longarm pointed toward the overturned locomotive at the bottom of the gulch far below. "They never had a chance."

The man choked with rage and sorrow. "Who did this?"

"We can't say for sure," Longarm hedged. "I haven't had the time to do much investigating. Mostly, we're just trying to keep the worst of the injured alive. Mister, that should also be your most immediate concern."

The tall man visibly reined in his emotions. "You're right! We'll get everyone on board and off to Cheyenne, where there's at least three good doctors."

Longarm and Martha joined the others to help the injured. Men with rifles were posted to watch over the train wreck, and it was decided that a second train would need to be sent up for the bodies.

"We'll be digging them out for a day or two and hunting for others scattered along this mountain," the tall man, whose name was Jim Allen, said. "I've seen a few train wrecks before, but nothing like this."

"Me neither," Longarm said wearily as he helped the last of the survivors on board the relief train.

31

It was a silent ride down the eastern slopes of the Laramie Mountains into the railhead town of Cheyenne. To their credit, when news of the train disaster spread across the city, hundreds of people rushed forward to offer aid, food, and shelter to the survivors. Newspaper reporters flocked around the injured, bedeviling them with questions that they could not answer.

"Deputy Long!" a newspaper man shouted, running up to join Longarm and Martha. "Were you on that ill-fated train?"

"I was," Longarm said, not wanting to talk to the man as he led Martha away from the train depot and yards.

"Can you explain what happened?" the newsman cried. "Nobody seems sure!"

"I'm not sure either."

"But you do agree that the train was robbed?"

"Yeah," Longarm said. "The train was robbed. The safe was blown from its hinges."

"Then it was probably the same gang that has been doing that for several years now, right?"

"That would be my guess."

The reporter's pencil scratched rapidly across his notebook. "And I understand that you were bringing Eli Wheat back to face the hangman."

Longarm sighed. "It seems that you already know about as much as I can tell you. Will you excuse us now? The lady is very tired."

"Miss Noble," the reporter said, turning to Martha. "I'm glad that you were not counted among the missing or dead."

"Yes, Herb. I'm very, very fortunate. It was a terrible ordeal and without our deputy marshal, I doubt half as many would have survived."

"Is that a fact?"

"No," Longarm said, "it is not. Everyone did all that they could to help those who were unable to help themselves. The survivors were those of us lucky enough not to be killed outright during the wreck."

Pencil scratching furiously, the reporter began to follow Longarm as he led the Martha away. "Deputy, if Eli Wheat escaped . . ."

"I don't know that for certain," Longarm said. "He might be lying on that mountainside or even down in the gulch, covered with rocks, snow, and wreckage."

"But you don't think so, do you?"

It wasn't a question, and Longarm had no compelling reason to answer in any event. However, if Eli could read a newspaper, Longarm wanted the man to know that he was going to be pursued to the very ends of the earth if necessary.

"No," Longarm said, "I don't think Eli is dead. And my hunch is that his escape did have something to do with the choice of this particular train to be dynamited. But since I can't be sure, I'll have to return to the wreck and do a thorough investigation."

"I see," the reporter said, flipping his notebook to a fresh page. "And I suppose that, if Eli is alive, you'll go after him?"

"You can bet your life on it!" Longarm took Martha's arm. "No more questions."

"My father's house is just up this street," Martha said. "He bought it a few years after I was married. When he died, he left it in my name."

"And now you'll live here and start that law practice?"

"That's my plan," Martha said without a great deal of enthusiasm. "I'm sure that my father left me a complete law library down at his offices. I've everything that I need to begin a practice except experience."

"Isn't there some kind of test or formal requirement?"

"There is, and I qualified before my marriage. It was my father's fondest dream that I should join his practice. He never cared that I wasn't a man. He said that I'd make a terrific attorney."

"I'm sure he was right," Longarm said as they approached a very stately two-story frame house. It was a beautiful home, though clearly it needed a little attention.

"Your father must have been very successful to buy such a nice house," Longarm said, lifting the gate and following Martha up to the front porch.

"He was." Martha sighed. "My father was a lawyer for the Union Pacific Railroad. He handled all litigation filed against them, and he saved the railroad thousands of dollars."

"You don't sound very impressed."

"There were some personal accident and injury cases where the railroad was clearly negligent and there should have been awards to some very desperate and deserving people."

"I see."

She studied him. "Yes, I imagine you do. I was an idealist then, and you saw a hint of that in me when we first met on the train yesterday. I was very critical of my father. Too critical. I went off to law school determined to balance the scales of justice in favor of the individual. I even kept the names of some of the plaintiffs that my father prevented from receiving fair awards."

"Do you still intend to right the wrongs of the past?"

"Absolutely. But this ordeal has shaken me and now, standing here on my father's porch, I feel as if I might somehow sully his name if I dig up the bones of the past."

"You should follow your conscience," Longarm advised. "If you have names of people who were robbed of fair compensation, you should right the wrong."

"Even if it might tarnish my father's name and reputation?"

"Your father is gone now. It's *your* reputation that you must establish, and I think you're going to do one hell of a good job of that."

Martha smiled. When she smiled, it was as if the sun peeked through a blanket of dark clouds and warmed a man's soul. "My father always hid a key on the porch," she said. "I doubt it will be hard to find."

It wasn't hard at all to find. In less than a minute, they had the key and were opening the door. At its threshold, Martha Noble hesitated.

"What's wrong?"

"I don't know. I just wish that my father and I had not quarreled so much. I wish that we hadn't fought the last time we were together."

"Put that behind you and look to your future. Obviously you've had some troubles with a bad marriage, and your father might not have been quite the knight in shining armor that a daughter would have hoped for. No matter. He worked for the railroad and he owed his allegiance to his employer."

"And not to justice?"

"Never mind that," Longarm said, gently pushing the young woman into the house and closing the door behind them.

Martha pirouetted around in a complete circle, her eyes missing nothing. "This house still smells like him," she finally said. "He smoked an unusually aromatic blend of Turkish pipe tobacco. You could follow it through the house and locate him with your eyes closed."

"It's a fine house and nicely furnished," Longarm said, admiring the expensive decor. "Your father had expensive tastes."

"Yes, he did."

Martha passed through the parlor and showed Longarm the library, kitchen, and other downstairs rooms that were primarily filled with French and Italian furniture and antiques. The ceramic floor tiles themselves were works of art, and the walls were covered with original artwork.

"I can't believe that no one has lived here since your father passed away."

"Didn't I mention that he only died two weeks ago?"

"No."

"Well, he did." Martha took Longarm's hand and led him to a beautiful staircase of polished walnut. "The bedrooms are upstairs. Would you like to see them?"

"I would," Longarm said, unable to hide his enthusiasm.

"Then come along."

She led him up the staircase and they entered the first bedroom, which had belonged to her father. Martha studied the room for a long time in silence, then backed out. When Longarm looked at her closely, he saw that her eyes were misted with tears.

"And this," she said, trying to put some lilt in her voice, "was my bedroom. He told me he kept it exactly the way it was when I left."

It was decorated in white and lavender. There were lace curtains and a bedspread to match. The furniture was heavy and very expensive.

"Nice bed," he offered.

"It's very comfortable." Martha walked over and sat down on her bed. When Longarm remained poised beside the door, she studied him for a moment, and then raised a finger and crooked it for him to come join her.

Longarm needed no further urging. Martha Noble was not the most beautiful woman he had ever seen or desired. She was pretty, but not classically beautiful. Her nose was a little too large, her lower jaw slightly undershot, and her figure less than perfect. But, after just twenty-four hours, he felt as if he had known her forever. She'd gone from being critical and naive to being sympathetic and understanding. Martha was not the same woman who had left Laramie on her way to confront the ghosts of her childhood in Cheyenne.

"Take me," she pleaded, clutching him tightly. "Smother me and make love to me as hard and as long as you can! Help me forget about last night."

"I can't do that," he said as he began to undress her. "Not really. But I can sweep away your doubts and fears for a while and take your mind off the bad things of the past. I can fill you with love."

"Then please do it. Only hurry!"

Longarm did not profess to understand women. He never had and he never would. Men who swore they understood the workings of the female mind were either

37

fools or liars. All that Longarm was certain of was his ability to make love to a woman so that, when he had to leave her, she was happy and satisfied.

Martha practically tore her own clothes off, and as soon as Longarm had his boots and pants off she was wild with desire. "Hurry!" she begged, reaching for his manhood. "I want you in me now!"

He pulled her silken-haired thighs wide apart, and when he reached down to guide his throbbing manhood into her honeypot, Martha was wet and ready. He felt her fingernails dig into his muscular buttocks as he plunged his rod into her with a series of hard, quick thrusts.

"Yes!" she cried, throwing her head back and then rolling it from side to side. "Oh, Custis, what would I have done without you up on that mountain?"

"You'd have survived," he grunted as their bodies pounded at each other like waves crashing against rocks. "You'd have survived!"

She found his mouth. Her tongue pushed between his teeth, and he could feel her body surging powerfully against his own. Spurred by her extraordinary passion, Longarm pinned her to the bed as his own body matched her intensity.

On and on they went, each lifting higher and higher. Finally, Martha threw back her head. A thin bead of perspiration covered her upper lip and her eyelids fluttered as she screamed, "Oh . . . oh!"

Longarm understood. He felt his own control crumble like a dam in a flood as his manhood spewed its torrent into her eager body. And for a few moments, he too forgot about the train wreck, the death, and the carnage.

She would not let him go the rest of the afternoon.

It was only when darkness fell on Cheyenne and his stomach was rumbling that she yielded to his plea for food and something to drink.

"I'll take you out to dinner," he said. "I doubt that there will be food in the house."

"You're all the food I need."

"I'm sorry," he told her, "but my stomach tells me that I need more than lovemaking."

"Then your stomach lies," she said with amusement.

"Besides, I can't stay here."

Martha blinked. "Why not?"

"Because you're trying to establish yourself in Cheyenne and it won't be easy. The last thing you want to do is to advertise a live-in lover. That will kill your chances with the respectable people of this town."

"To hell with them."

"No," Longarm said, climbing out of her bed. "You can't say that. You need their support, Martha. And you deserve their support. You came here to make some atonement for your father, and I'm not going to be a part of spoiling that."

She laughed softly. "Why, you're a real moralist! Who would have believed this conversation? Longarm, I'm offering you . . . everything. I want to marry you."

It was his turn to laugh. "Marry and keep me? Thanks, but no thanks."

"I didn't mean that the way it sounded. Of course I wouldn't 'keep you.' I heard Mr. Ashmore offer you a job with the Bank of Wyoming. You could accept his offer."

"He died in the wreck," Longarm said quietly.

"Oh." Martha cleared her throat. "I'd forgotten. All

right then, go to his bank and tell them what Mr. Ashmore offered you. Ask for the job and then we'll be married."

"Just like that?"

"Not just like that!" Martha bounced out of bed without a stitch of clothing. She threw her arms around Longarm's neck and hugged him. "Custis, more than anything, I want to be your wife. I want to marry my hero."

Longarm disengaged himself. "Martha, you're a beautiful young woman and you're going to marry again. And you're going to be more successful than your father. But we're not going to get married."

"Why not?"

"Because," he said simply, "I don't want to get married. What I want and have to do is find Eli Wheat and the men that derailed that train and caused so many good and innocent people to die—some of them slowly and in great pain."

Martha stepped back. "All right. So we don't get married until you deliver Mr. Wheat and his friends to the hangman. Then can we marry?"

"I like my work."

"Your work will be your death! Sooner or later, someone will ambush or shoot you in the back. Or your horse will spill you over a cliff or something terrible will happen."

"I don't think so," he said, gentling her fears. "I lead a sort of charmed life."

"I don't believe that for a moment. Look at the scars you carry on your body! You look like you've been stitched up in five or six places, and I recognize a bullet wound when I see one."

"I'm like a cat with nine lives," he said with a wink.

"And with eight of them gone!"

Longarm's stomach rumbled in protest. "Martha, let's go out and get something to eat."

Her shoulders slumped. "Just tell me that you'll come back when you've captured or killed Eli and his gang. That's all I ask."

"It may take some time and some doing."

"You'll do it. Promise me, please?"

"All right," he conceded, "I'll come back."

"Good! My father was close friends with Edward's father, who founded the Bank of Wyoming. I'll speak to the old gentleman tomorrow and ask him to hold that job opening."

"Now—"

"Just in case!" Martha added quickly. "Just in case."

Longarm dipped his chin in reluctant agreement. Martha reached down and began to play with his flaccid rod, and he decided to wait a few minutes before getting dressed, just in case.

Chapter 4

The next morning, Longarm paid a visit to the telegraph office to send a message to his boss, U.S. Marshal Billy Vail, back in Denver.

"All right, Deputy," the telegraph operator said, pencil poised over pad. "Shoot."

"To Marshal Vail." Longarm paused, gathered his thoughts, and began to dictate. "Prisoner Eli Wheat escaped custody during train derailment near Laramie Summit. Stop. Many passengers killed and injured and mail car robbed. Stop. Appears to be same gang that has derailed other U.P. trains. Stop. Going after Eli Wheat and train wreck gang. Stop. Need one hundred and fifty dollars for outfit and travel expenses. Stop."

"Don't you want me to add your name?"

"He'll know who the telegram is from."

"Terrible thing that happened up there," the operator said, shaking his head. "I knew most of the train crew that died. They were all good men. Didn't deserve something like that to happen to 'em."

"Neither did the passengers."

"Mr. Ashmore left a wife and three small children," the telegraph operator added quietly. "I tell you, there's going to be some sad grievin' in this town for a good long while."

"I know. All that I can do is to try and bring whoever caused that train wreck to a quick and final justice. Which reminds me, I need to buy a horse."

"Bob's Livery is the best place to go. He's a good, honest man and takes care of his customers. I guarantee that he'll treat you right."

"Thanks," Longarm said, before asking for directions. Fifteen minutes later, he was looking at a pen of saddle horses over a split-rail fence.

"Now that bay gelding with the blaze on his face is one of the better animals," Bob said. "He's an older horse, but steady and sound."

"What about that dun?"

"I wouldn't trust his legs. Bought him from a horse trader for next to nothing because I figured he might have some fundamental unsoundness."

"And the palomino?"

"Hard-mouthed and stubborn. He's half bronc."

"What about that tall sorrel with the white star on his forehead?"

Bob smiled. "You've a keen eye for good horseflesh. Cowboy rode him into town and made a big fuss over the horse, but he wanted cash real bad. Said he had a sister in Omaha that needed his help and he had to have some cash for travel. I paid forty dollars for the animal after watching the cowboy ride for about ten minutes. Seems like a good horse and the cowboy said he was fast and had endurance. He's a little big-headed and Roman-nosed."

"That doesn't matter to me," Longarm said. "I like his looks and the size. How much do you want?"

"For you, same as I paid. And for a total of fifty dollars, I'll throw in an old saddle, bridle, and blanket."

"How about a new set of shoes? The only reason I caught up with Eli Wheat this last time was because his unshod horses went lame."

"You're right. I shoe my own horses and I'll do the sorrel. For five more dollars, you've got a freshly shod horse *and* I'll toss in a rope, halter, and set of hobbles. You'd have everything you need to catch Eli and his murdering friends."

"Fifty-five dollars total."

"That's right."

Longarm knew that, if the horse was as sound and sensible an animal as he appeared to be, it was a very fair price. "Saddle him up and let me ride him around."

"Sure!"

The sorrel was light-mouthed, quick-reining, and alert. Longarm was no cowboy, but he could recognize a horse that was well trained and eager to please. "I'll take him. I'm expecting a telegram and wired money this afternoon."

"He'll have a fresh pair of shoes and be ready when you are," the liveryman promised.

Satisfied that he had bought himself a good horse, Longarm next went to the general store, where he purchased food, a bedroll, supplies, and a heavy, waterproof canvas sack in which to carry everything.

"I'm also going to need a pair of woolen underwear and a leather coat," he told the proprietor.

"We can fix you right up," the man said with a somber expression. "And I'll tell you something else, Deputy. I'm not going to take a cent of profit."

"You're not?"

"No. I'm selling everything to you at cost because I want you to catch and bring those men to justice. The engineer on board that train that died was one of my best friends. So you find those killers and give them no quarter, hear me?"

"I hear you," Longarm said. "And that brings me to the last thing I need, which is a rifle. I haven't got a lot of money, so if you've got something used but serviceable and that shoots straight, that would be fine."

"You want a .30-30 carbine?"

"Maybe something heavier."

"I've a fine Remington Rolling-block .50 I could offer at a good price."

"That's an excellent rifle, but I'm in need of something that holds more than one shot."

"I see. How about a Winchester Model 1873? I've a battered but serviceable fifteen-shot with a twenty-four-inch barrel. It's heavier than the .30-30, being a .44-40 caliber."

"Let me see it."

The rifle's stock had been broken and crudely repaired with nails and wire, and then covered with tightly stretched rawhide. The Winchester wasn't anything for looks, but the ugly stock felt solid and Longarm figured that he might need a fifteen-shot weapon with reaching power.

"How much?"

"Ten dollars." The man smiled. "That's what I paid for it. Bought it off a Cheyenne, but not before I tested it for accuracy. It shoots straight and the action is smooth."

"Sold."

Longarm left the general store and returned to Martha's house. She wasn't home, so he packed his things, put on his new clothes, and headed back into town. After receiving directions, Longarm ended up at the fancy law offices of Noble, Evans, and Black.

"Excuse me," he said to a clerk wearing a green eyeshade. "I'm looking for Miss Noble."

"She's in conference with Mr. Evans and Mr. Black. If you could come back later . . ."

"I don't think so," Longarm said, pushing past the clerk.

"Hey, you can't go in there!"

But Longarm was already "in there," pushing open the door to the private office, and surprising Martha and two older men.

"Custis!"

"I apologize for this sudden and unannounced interruption," Longarm said, "but I'm about to leave Cheyenne. Martha, I thought I ought to say good-bye."

Martha's smile died and she jumped to her feet. "You're leaving so soon?"

"I need to get on the outlaws' trail," Longarm said. "If it snows again, the tracks are lost. Every hour I delay is an hour that it will be tough to make up."

"Any idea where they might have gone?" one of the well-dressed men asked.

"No," Longarm admitted. "They seem to have the ability to vanish into thin air. They might even have dispersed in all directions. Today, given the telegraph and so many law enforcement agencies, a really smart gang comes

46

together only when they have a stage or a train to rob."

"That would make it tough to apprehend them," the other lawyer said.

"Damned tough," Longarm agreed, not able to take his eyes off Martha, who looked beautiful and very competent in a black pleated skirt and white silk blouse.

Martha took his arm. "Gentlemen, you must excuse me for a few minutes while I say good-bye to my friend."

The lawyers did not looked pleased, but nodded in agreement. "We'll be waiting, Miss Noble."

"It'll only be a moment," she replied, leading Longarm out of their office.

Once they were out on the board sidewalk, Martha slipped her arms around Longarm's waist. Tears made her eyes glisten. "It just occurred to me that I may never see you again."

"I swear that I'll return."

Her lower lip trembled. "But not to take that job or to get married."

"I can't say what I'll do for the future, Martha. All I know for sure is that I've already got a big job to do."

"You don't know anything about this bunch and you don't even know how many there are."

"I'll know more when I pick up their trail," he said. "A lot more."

Martha laid her head against his chest. "I'm scared for you, Custis. What if you get killed?"

"Then your life goes on just as it did before we met two days ago."

"It seems like we've known each other for years. I can't imagine not having known you."

47

Longarm hugged her tightly. "Martha, I have to go now. Stretching out a good-bye never does any good."

She released him and stepped back. "I've told Mr. Evans and Mr. Black that they can either buy me out of their partnership or bring me into the firm that my father founded as an equal partner. It seems that they're having a very difficult time with that decision, but I'm sure that they will make the right choice. You see, they both have suffered investment losses and don't have much cash on hand."

"I wish you a good start on your new life," Longarm said before kissing her and then turning on his heel and marching on down the boardwalk.

"I'll be waiting for you!" she called.

When Longarm reached the telegraph office, there was a telegram from his boss that read: GET THE BASTARDS—DEAD OR ALIVE. Billy had also wired a check for two hundred dollars, which told Longarm better than words that he was supposed to stay out on the trail no matter how long it took to bring Eli Wheat and the train-robbing gang to justice.

"Your boss sounds pretty upset," the telegraph operator said. "I never got a telegraph like that before."

"Marshal Vail means business, all right," Longarm agreed.

A few minutes later he collected the cash at the bank, and then went to collect his horse. It was nearly noon before Longarm was ready to ride.

"I hope you shoot them," Bob said as Longarm mounted the sorrel. "I hope you kill every last one."

"My job is to take them alive, if possible, and bring them to trial."

48

"If you do that," the liveryman said, "I'll come down to Denver to watch them dance on the gallows."

"You'd be welcome," Longarm said as he reined his horse west and put it into a gallop toward the nearby Laramie Mountains.

It was late afternoon and the snow was almost gone when Longarm rode the tough sorrel gelding up to the site of the train wreck. Union Pacific crews were everywhere cleaning up debris and searching for more bodies. Jim Allen saw Longarm, and came over to greet him.

"More bodies?" Longarm asked.

"Two. I think we have them all now. It's a wonder that everyone wasn't killed."

"Yeah." Longarm glanced up the line toward the summit. "Did you see any sign of an explosion?"

"I haven't had time to look. All my attention has been down the side of this mountain. That big locomotive will rest in that gulch forever."

"Let's take a look up the track and see if we can find out why it derailed," Longarm said, reining up-slope.

He rode about two hundred yards back up the track, and dismounted to stare at the great pit where dynamite had exploded to twist the tracks like hairpins.

"Holy cow!" Allen said, catching up. "They must have used a *barrel* of dynamite."

"That's right," Longarm said. "They weren't scrimping, that's for sure. And they brought a wagon along to carry off whatever they could find, including the safe in the mail car in case they couldn't blast it open."

"At least it should be easy tracking them," the railroad supervisor offered hopefully.

Longarm handed the sorrel's reins to Allen and began to study the signs. He saw boot marks and cigarette butts and plenty of horse tracks just up-slope and behind a pile of rocks.

"They didn't need to hide, but they must have been trying to get out of the weather as they waited for the train."

"I wish they'd have frozen solid," Allen spat out.

Longarm spent another fifteen minutes studying signs. There wasn't a lot to see because the snow had covered the ground, then melted, leaving everything indistinct. He wasn't even sure how many men had been involved.

"You find anything real important?" Allen asked.

"Afraid not."

"Too bad. Looks like they had a wagon that should be plenty easy to follow."

Longarm's eyes followed the wagon tracks. He was very sure that he would find the wagon abandoned somewhere up in the mountains. Furthermore, he was expecting that the tracks of the horsemen he followed would splinter into small groups.

"I've got about an hour of daylight left is all," Longarm said. "Best make use of it."

"Good luck, Deputy. I wish there was something that I could do to help you. There must be more lawmen coming."

"I prefer to work alone," Longarm said. "But you can bet that railroad detectives, Pinkerton agents, and other federal marshals are on their way. Thing of it is, I was on that train and it was my prisoner that escaped."

"Yeah," Allen said. "And it was *my* men and passengers that died."

Longarm tugged his Stetson low over his eyes and rode on, following the wagon and its tracks. The gang of train robbers was smart enough to travel single file in front of the wagon and its team of horses so that it was impossible to read how many there were. However, Longarm thought that he was following at least a half dozen—and perhaps many more. If there was any good news at all, it was that so many men would attract attention and be remembered by anyone who saw them—anyone, that is, who lived to report a sighting.

Chapter 5

As sundown fired the western sky, Longarm crested the backbone of the Laramie Mountains and began to search for a campsite. There was a cold wind sweeping through the pines, and Longarm sought a heavy stand of timber to cut the wind. At least, he thought, there was no sign of another storm on the horizon. If there had been, Longarm would have pushed on by starlight, following the tracks all night if possible.

To Longarm's surprise, the outlaws' trail led to an old, abandoned cabin where the train robbers had spent their first night. In addition to the cabin, there was a sturdy pole corral. Before penning his weary sorrel, Longarm once again searched for any bit of knowledge that would serve him in the future. The buckboard used by the gang had been left behind and it held no clues.

All that Longarm discovered after an inspection of the corral was a horse's hoofprint revealing a broken right shoe. That, and a cigarette butt that was wrapped in an unusual pale yellow paper that Longarm had not seen before. Otherwise, the corral, the cabin, and the surrounding yard offered not a shred of evidence that would help to identify the train robbers.

"These boys are pretty careful," Longarm muttered as he hauled his bedroll and gear into the cabin and then set about to make himself a small fire on a stone hearth.

That night, the wind blew hard and cold. Longarm slept poorly, and was up before dawn to saddle his horse. He could not exactly say why, but he was sure that the train robbers were heading for Laramie. No doubt they would filter into the busy town in ones and twos in order to avoid drawing attention to themselves.

Longarm's hunch was confirmed a few hours later when the tracks indicated that the gang had gathered about a mile west of town, then separated into a number of small groups, all moving toward Laramie from different directions and probably all staggered so that they'd arrive over a period of several hours.

"But then what?" Longarm asked himself aloud. "Do they live in Laramie? Work on ranches in the vicinity? Or will they drift on down the line singly and in pairs, only to regroup and plot another train robbery?"

These were the questions that plagued Longarm as he approached Laramie. Unlike Cheyenne, Laramie had existed before the arrival of the Union Pacific Railroad. The town had been named after Jacques LaRamie, a Frenchman who had first passed through this beautiful country while trapping beaver for the American Fur Company. Following his path had come the emigrants, soldiers, and fortune-seekers, many tracing the old Cherokee Trail. Fort Sanders, just to the South, had offered protection to the Overland Stage Line, and later for the predominantly Irish survey and construction crews of the Union Pacific.

Longarm had always liked this town, which was nestled against the western base of the mountains. Laramie was picturesque, and could boast of its wild and exciting history. Vigilantes had played a big part in the early years, and now Laramie was home to not only the railroad employees, but also to the cowboys, loggers, and even miners who worked this ruggedly beautiful part of Wyoming.

When the tracks he followed had begun to branch into many splintered pairs, just as Longarm had anticipated, he'd made sure that he followed the horse with the broken shoe. It was an easy track to follow, and Longarm was pinning all his hopes on being able to locate the animal and then its owner. If he could just nab one of the train robbers, he might be able to get a confession leading to the arrest of the entire gang.

The track he had chosen to follow, however, became obliterated at the edge of Laramie, where it was trampled and churned under by heavy wagon and horse traffic. Longarm sighed with resignation. He knew he had been unrealistic in his hope that the track would be plainly visible all the way into town, but still, he needed some break in this case.

At the edge of town, Longarm drew his horse to a standstill and considered his options for a moment. Actually, there was only one—he had to find the horse with the broken shoe before it was reshod and his only clue was lost.

"Best go see the town's blacksmiths," he said to himself, thinking that the train robber had to be aware that his horse needed to be reshod.

Unfortunately, there were three blacksmiths operating

in Laramie. Longarm made it a point to visit them all. The first blacksmith had just closed his business and moved to California, but the second blacksmith was hard at work when Longarm arrived on his sweaty sorrel.

"Morning," he said to the man, who as in the middle of shoeing a horse. "I'm Deputy U.S. Marshal Custis Long. Fella up the street told me that your name is Ned Rowe."

"Whoever he was talks too damned much."

The horse being shod was acting up and the blacksmith was clearly angry. "Can't you see that I'm right in the middle of a horse that's about to raise holy hell!"

"I can see that," Longarm said. "So why don't you put his foot down and step back for a minute. I've got a couple of questions I'd like to ask."

"You may be a federal officer, but you don't pay my rent," the blacksmith growled. "So if you got anything to say, say it while I'm tacking on this shoe. I ain't got no time to waste on free talk, Deputy."

"Mister, I don't see how you stay in business with such a chip on your shoulder."

The blacksmith glared at Longarm. "If you had to shoe as many ornery horses and mules as I do each day to make a living, you'd have better things to do than to waste people's time. Now, I ain't seen your badge yet."

Longarm gritted his teeth to keep from increasing the immediate dislike he and the blacksmith had taken to each other. He summoned up enough patience to show the man his badge, which he did not routinely keep on display. Like most things, Longarm had a good reason for keeping his badge out of sight most of the time. He'd known desperate and hunted outlaws to actually draw their guns and shoot badge-toters without warning.

"That satisfy you, or do I have to find your sheriff and make things ugly?"

"Whoa!" the blacksmith yelled, jumping back as the horse he was shoeing tried to rear. "Goddamn you jug-headed sonofabitch!"

"You haven't got much patience, have you?" Longarm drawled as the blacksmith jerked on the horse's lead rope and tried to discipline it to shoeing.

The blacksmith took a swing at the horse, but missed and crashed to the ground.

Suppressing a smile, Longarm said, "Mr. Rowe, it's plain to see that the animal is scared. Give him a few minutes to settle down and talk to him gentle and I'll bet he'd behave himself. Save you both some considerable wear and tear."

"Do you want to shoe this miserable bastard?"

"Nope."

"Then what the hell *do* you want?"

Longarm could see that this man was in a bad state of mind and nothing but a fight and a good whipping would correct Ned Rowe's poor way of thinking. "Well, to begin with, I want to know if that horse was brought in with a broken right shoe."

"Nope." Rowe yanked on the horse's lead rope again. "So why are you asking such a foolish question?"

"I'm looking for a horse with a broken right shoe. Probably a right foreshoe."

"If you find the animal and it's got any sense, send it my way," Rowe growled. "I can always use the business."

Longarm dismounted and dropped to one knee. He dug

his pocket knife out of his Levi's and said, "Come here and take a look at what I'm about to show you."

Rowe started to say something, then clamped his mouth shut as if he thought better of it. "What the hell are you going to do?"

"If someone brings in an animal with a shoe like this," Longarm said, sketching a horseshoe to indicate how the track he had followed down from the cabin had appeared, "then I'll pay you ten dollars to alert me."

The anger drained out of the blacksmith's square face, and was replaced by a look of cunning. "Say now, Deputy, this wouldn't have anything to do with that train wreck up at the summit, would it?"

"Ten dollars," Longarm repeated. "And if it leads to the arrest of the men I want, there could be a whole lot more in reward money."

The blacksmith's entire demeanor underwent a transformation. "I'll keep it in mind, Marshal! My back aches and I can't pay my bills, what with the hard times we're in right now. How much is the reward for them train robbers?"

"I didn't say anything about any train robbers."

"You didn't have to. I'm not stupid, and neither is anyone else in this town. We're expecting a whole raft of lawmen to come sniffin' around looking for that bunch of murderin' sonofabitches."

"Well," Longarm said, "I was on that train and my prisoner escaped and a lot of passengers died. So I have a personal need to get my hands on those men first. Is that clear?"

The blacksmith was not as tall as Longarm, but he was more muscular. "Hey," he said, "I'm on *your* side! If someone brings a horse in with a shoe like you've drawn, I'll beat a hot trail to you. Count on it!"

"I'll be staying just up the street at the Outpost Hotel," Longarm said. "But I don't think that I'll be there more than a day or two."

"If this horse that you're looking for was ridden all the way down from the summit with a broken shoe, I'm surprised he hasn't gone lame yet."

"Me too."

"You gonna go to my competitor with the same offer?"

"Sure, why not?"

"No reason," the blacksmith said quickly. "But he's blind and drunk most of the time. He won't help you."

"I'll be looking pretty hard for myself," Longarm informed the man. "But if I was riding a horse with a broken shoe, I'd take notice and get him shod right away. That's why I came to you first thing."

"Much obliged! And hey, what about your horse, Deputy? Looks like he could use a new set of irons."

"Hell," Longarm drawled, "he was just shod in Cheyenne yesterday."

Ned Rowe scratched his belly and turned back to the horse he was working on. He jerked hard on the rope, and the animal backed away in fear. "All right, jug-head! You settled down yet?"

"Yes, sir, Ned, you sure got a fine way with horses," Longarm said cryptically as he reined his sorrel on down the street to find the other blacksmith.

"Go to hell, Deputy!"

At the corner of the street, Longarm glanced back and saw that Ned Rowe was watching him closely. Did the man know something that he wasn't telling about the gang? Longarm hadn't a clue. Most likely, Rowe didn't know anything. He didn't seem the sort to ride with an outlaw gang. Still, he might know someone who did. Or just as likely, he might even know who owned the horse with the broken right shoe, and might even decide that he could use his information for a share of the train's bounty.

Yes, sir, Longarm thought, Ned Rowe had the cunning look of a person who would have no qualms about playing both sides against the middle in order to gain a windfall. The man would definitely bear watching and another visit.

The other blacksmith was far more cooperative. His name was Jimmie Jeter and he was a short, balding man considerably past his prime for this hard and dangerous work. In addition to being a blacksmith, he ran a livery stable.

"Sure, Deputy, I'll watch for a horse like that. And how much did you say the reward might be?"

"I didn't say," Longarm told the man. "But it could be a considerable amount of money."

"Have you already visited Ned Rowe?"

"I have."

"Too bad."

"Why?"

Jimmy shrugged. With one worn boot heel hooked over a bottom fence rail and his arms hooked over the top fence rail, he was as relaxed as Ned Rowe had been angry.

"Well, Deputy Long, it might interest you to know that Ned's brother was hanged for horse thieving about two years ago. His father was a cattle rustler and hanged about three years before that. He's got a younger sister who's a whore in Rock Springs, and his mother shot herself last winter."

"Sounds like a sorry family."

"The Rowes are trash and always have been. Ned is as crooked as a dog's hind leg."

"I see." Longarm hooked his own heel over the rail and gazed off toward the distant mountains. "Jimmie, are you suggesting that Ned might be mixed up with the train robberies?"

"Oh," Jimmie drawled, "I'm not suggesting anything. He's mean and drinks too damn much. He's awful with horses and not much of a shoer, but I sure wouldn't want to see him get into trouble."

"Ned says that his business isn't very good."

"Course it isn't! Word gets around. He'll whip a horse with his shoeing file. He's lamed a few by cutting them to the quick because he gets angry and impatient. I'm not just saying that because he's my only competitor, Deputy."

"I'm sure you're not."

"The truth of the matter is," Jimmie said, chewing on a stem of alfalfa, "Ned has a wild streak. Sometimes he just closes his shop, saddles a horse, and rides off for a few days at a time."

"Any idea where he might go?"

"Nope. I'm told that Ned rides over to Cheyenne and gets drunk. My wife thinks that Ned has a whore over there that he's fond of dallying with."

"What do *you* think Ned does?"

"I think he's foolin' around with more than whiskey and bad women," Jimmie said.

Longarm waited for a further explanation. When it

became obvious that it would not be forthcoming, he said, "Why do you think he's up to something illegal?"

"Because Ned always returns with more money than he leaves with."

"Maybe he goes to Cheyenne and shoes a few horses."

Jimmie chuckled softly. "Hell, Deputy! You've got a fine sense of humor, don't you?"

Longarm hadn't meant for his remark to be humorous. "Watch for that horse with the broken shoe, Jimmie. If it shows up, get word to me right away at the hotel or track me down here in town."

"What about the sheriff? You going to be working with him on this?"

"I've never met the man."

"He's new," Jimmie said. "I don't trust him any more than I do Ned Rowe."

Longarm frowned. "Jimmie, despite your easygoing ways, I'm beginning to wonder if you're just naturally a suspicious kind of fella."

Jimmie laughed outright. "Deputy, if you think *I'm* suspicious, just you trot on over to pay your respects to Sheriff Cotton. He'll make *you* suspicious too, and he's the sheriff!"

"I will pay him a visit."

"Do yourself a favor."

"What's that?"

The smile died on Jimmie's wrinkled face. "Let's just keep the broken horseshoe thing to ourselves for a few days. Never mind the fool sheriff. If the horse comes to town and its owner knows anything about my reputation, he'll bring the animal here."

"And if he brings the horse to Ned?"

"Then I'd say you have two of the train robbers caught dead to rights."

Longarm nodded. He wasn't sure that he believed Jimmie, but the man's suspicions sure needed investigating. And being forewarned about Laramie's new sheriff was something that Longarm appreciated. As a federal officer, he often had to work in cooperation with the local authorities. Sometimes it worked, often it did not. Sheriffs and town marshals had a tendency to be pretty closed-mouthed, and they often did not appreciate having a federal officer who might show them up as incompetent working in their jurisdiction.

"Keep an eye out and feed my horse well," Longarm said, untying his saddlebags.

"You can count on Jimmie," the blacksmith said cheerfully. "I got the best eyes in Laramie when it comes to a horse's feet."

Longarm believed the man, and he had a hunch that if the horse he sought were anywhere in Laramie, Jimmie would find it first.

Chapter 6

"Sheriff Cotton?"

"At your service," the chubby man with a shiny star and boots to match said as he eased out of his desk chair. "But most people call me Ike."

"I'm Deputy U.S. Marshal Custis Long. I'm a federal officer working out of the Denver office."

Ike Cotton's smile dimmed a little. He sucked in his gut and puffed out his chest. "Take a load off your feet, Deputy. You been in Laramie long?"

"No. I just rode in. But I was on the train that was derailed a few days ago and sent down the mountainside just beyond the summit."

"I heard all about that," Cotton said. "Of course, I couldn't go up there and investigate. My own deputy quit—you aren't lookin' for a job, are you?"

"No."

Cotton settled into his overstuffed desk chair. He was of average height, smooth-faced, and flabby. His hands were delicate, and his thin blond hair was slicked against his scalp while his mustache was waxed at the tips. With the benefit of money, Sheriff Cotton would have been a dandy.

"Well," Cotton blustered, "that's too bad. I could use an experienced deputy. One that knows that there is more to being a lawman than just sitting behind a desk with your feet up in the air."

"I'm sure you could," Longarm said drily.

"So," Cotton said, buffing his badge with the cuff of his sleeve. "What exactly can I do for you?"

"As you might imagine," Longarm began, "I'm looking for the men who derailed and robbed that Union Pacific passenger train. I have reason to believe that Eli Wheat— a prisoner I was transporting back to Denver—was a member of that gang and escaped with them."

"Hmmm. Interesting. Unfortunately, I've never met this Wheat fella, but if you want to give me his description, I'll sure enough keep a sharp eye peeled for him."

Longarm was not impressed. "It's damned unlikely that Wheat would ride into Laramie. He was pretty well known and would be easily recognized by too many people. What I am looking for is anyone who has caught your eye as being a stranger and having a lot of money."

"Well," Cotton said, placing his boots up on his desk and lacing his fingers behind his head, "as you know, this is a railroad town. We get a lot of folks passing through and some of them do have a considerable amount of money."

Cotton chuckled, then winked conspiratorially. "Money that our local gambling halls and painted ladies take great pains to extract and invest in our local economy. If you know what I mean."

"I know what you mean," Longarm replied, deciding that this man was a complete fool. "Did you see any strangers enter Laramie in the last day or two on horseback?"

Cotton dropped his folksy facade and put his boots on the floor. "Now listen here, Deputy. Laramie is a damn busy town and I'm a busy man. There are no less than fifty big ranches within a hard day's ride, and all of them are constantly sending cowboys in to raise hell or to buy supplies. I couldn't begin to keep my eye on the comings or goings of all them cowboys and line riders."

"The men I seek," Longarm said, thinking that Jimmie Jeter's assessment of this incompetent sheriff had been right on the money, "would have been riding hard-used horses and wouldn't have necessarily had the look of cowboys."

"If they were on horseback, then how would a man know if they were cowboys or not?"

Longarm gave up. It was clear to him that further conversation with Sheriff Ike Cotton would be a complete waste of time. "Well," he said, coming to his feet, "that's a real good question."

Slightly mollified by this response, Cotton relaxed. "How can I help you, Deputy? I don't like other lawmen nosin' around in my town, but we are in the same line of work and we have to help each other."

"That's the way I see it."

"So what do you know?" Cotton asked point-blank.

"Not a damn thing," Longarm said. "I followed the outlaws to Laramie and—"

Cotton's double chins sagged. "They rode into *my* town?"

"Yes."

"How many?" Cotton exclaimed, almost falling out of his desk chair.

"I couldn't exactly say." Longarm frowned. "Somewhere between six and a dozen would be my guess."

"I'd have noticed them if they came here."

"They came in one and two at a time to avoid your notice," Longarm explained, saying what should have been obvious. "And for all I know, they might already have left the same way."

Cotton sighed with audible relief. "I sure hope so."

"I don't," Longarm said. "I hope they're here to the last man so that I can track them down."

"How do you propose to do that?"

"I'll just keep looking. And I know you will too."

"But I don't even know what to look for!" Cotton raised his hands, then let them fall helplessly to his sides. "You've got to give me something to work with."

"Look closely at every stranger," Longarm said. "See if their horses are wearing local brands or not. Ask them what ranches they are working. Find out if they're known by people hereabouts or are judged by the townspeople to be newcomers. And try to see if they've got any money."

"Cowboys coming into Laramie always have money to spend."

"Yeah, I'm sure that they do," Longarm said, "but these boys will have quite a lot of money."

"How much did they get?"

"All the U.P. would say was that there was several thousand dollars cash in their mail car safe. There may also have been other valuables and documents. Sheriff,

66

my advice is that, if anyone tries to cash in jewelry, stocks, or such, let me know."

"I sure will!" The sheriff licked his lips and wrung his hands. "You know how poor the pay is for a lawman—especially on the local level."

"No one forced you to take the job."

"No one else wanted the job for fifty dollars a month!" Cotton looked away for a moment, beat the anger out of his voice, and said, "What's the reward money like on these train robbers, and particularly this Eli Wheat fella?"

"It's not been posted yet, but I imagine there is already at least a hundred dollar reward posted on Eli."

"Well, I'll sure be on the lookout for them," the sheriff said brightly. "And we should keep in close touch."

"I'll stop by at least once a day," Longarm said, though he knew that this sheriff would be pumping him for information and not gather a shred of his own. "I'm staying at the Outpost Hotel."

"Nice place! Best in town. I eat in their dining room on every payday." The sheriff dredged up a sad and slightly hopeful smile. "That's only once a month, but to tell you the truth, I'd give anything to eat there more often."

Longarm ignored the thinly veiled hint at a free meal and headed out the door. "I'm sure they like having you just as often as possible, Sheriff Cotton."

He checked into the Outpost Hotel, which mostly catered to the big game hunters that came to the West to kill trophy-sized buffalo, elk, moose, and grizzly bear. The Outpost Hotel was the finest establishment in Laramie, and beyond the means of a federal officer, but Longarm was dirty and tired, had spent too much time on the trail, and was in no mood to save the government money. Besides, the Outpost would send his expense vouchers into Marshal Vail's office, allowing Longarm to hang onto his travel expense money in case of an emergency. That was why he stayed there whenever he was passing through town.

"Hello, Deputy Long," the tall, elegant proprietor said with genuine warmth. "Welcome back!"

"Thank you, Earl. I just wish that the circumstances weren't so grim."

Earl pushed the register book at Longarm. "Forgive me for saying so, but you look very tired. I suppose that you've been working night and day on that train derailment and robbery."

"Not nights," Longarm admitted. "But I was on that train when it went down the mountainside. It was a miracle that any of us survived because it was very bad."

"I heard the locomotive rolled for half a mile."

"Not quite, but it's there forever. Fortunately, most of the coaches were light enough that they broke up on the mountainside instead of rolling all the way to the bottom of the gulch. Ours caught on some rocks or I wouldn't be here today."

"I can't imagine anything like that," Earl said. "It must have been a nightmare."

"It was. There were no dead children, thank God. But there were some ladies that died."

Earl's voice shook with passion. "I hope you find the . . . murderers who committed that terrible act."

"I'll find them," Longarm vowed. "In fact, I think they might even be in Laramie right now."

"No!" Earl whispered, leaning forward with an expression of pure amazement.

"I mean it. Earl, I've been a regular customer for three or four years, haven't I?"

"Oh, yes, sir!"

"Well, I want you to keep a sharp eye out for rough men with fast money."

"This isn't the kind of a place such men would frequent, Deputy Long."

"We can't be too sure of that. Sometimes when a man gets a lot of fast money, they step out of their normal haunts and try to show a little class."

"I've seen that happen," Earl admitted. "Usually they've just gotten lucky at cards. They rarely stay for more than one night as our guest and they never return."

"That would be the kind of men I'm looking for. There is one other small thing."

Earl leaned forward. "And that is?"

"I found this cigarette butt in a corral up on the mountain. I can't say for sure, but I'm confident that it was smoked by one of the train robbers."

Longarm showed Earl the unusual cigarette paper. "Have you ever seen anything like it before?"

Earl did not deign to touch the cigarette butt, but his eyebrows jerked upward and when he glanced up at Longarm, his face was animated with excitement. "That's a *British* cigarette. It's called Royal Crown. It's rather expensive, and the tobacco is said to be of the highest quality. You won't find a working cowboy buying those cigarettes."

"Where can they be bought?"

"At certain tobacco shops. They would be sold at a tobacco shop in Cheyenne, and there are two tobacconists who sell them in Denver."

"I see." Longarm studied the butt. "Look, Earl, if you see anyone smoking these things, I want to know about it right away."

"We always have a few guests here who smoke Royal Crown cigarettes. But I'd not want them to be . . . accosted."

"I promise I'll be discreet. They'll likely never even realize I was investigating their whereabouts on the night that train was wrecked."

Longarm leaned forward across the desk. "Earl, you know that I'm not a wealthy man but that I am generous."

"You have always been *very* generous to us. You are one of my favorite guests. I mean that in all honesty."

Longarm knew that this was going to cost him thirty or forty dollars, but if the broken horseshoe proved to be a dead-end trail, this was his only hope and it was no time to be pinching pennies.

"I'll continue to be generous," Longarm said, patting Earl's shoulder. "Now, if I could have a room and a hot bath?"

"At once. At once!"

Longarm dined in the hotel that night and he ate very, very well. Buffalo steak, sourdough bread, fresh trout sautéed in mushrooms, asparagus, and a peach cobbler with cool, sweet cream. Longarm even allowed himself to finish off the meal with a good cigar and two glasses of French brandy.

"I haven't eaten so well," he confessed to the waiter, "since I was here last. Compliments to Chef Pierre."

"He knows it is you, Mr. Long, and so he made everything extra special."

"He did indeed."

The waiter beamed, and Longarm settled back with contentment. He'd been shaved, and was wearing a fresh change of clothes and underwear. He almost felt civilized, and was in no hurry to leave the warm and pleasant surroundings where he had spent many a happy evening.

"Hello!" the woman purred, leaning over the table so that the upper portions of her large breasts dangled like overripe melons. "My dear, dear deputy. I didn't expect you to be back so soon!"

"Well, Milly," he replied, "neither did I. But there was this train wreck on the mountain just to the east of us, and ever since my life has sort of gone to hell."

"You look pretty happy right now." Milly slid into the chair and laid a familiar hand on Longarm's muscular thigh. "I think that I can make you look even happier with almost no effort at all."

"Milly, you vixen!"

"Buy me a drink?"

"Sure."

Longarm ordered them both brandy, and then he told Milly about the train wreck, Eli Wheat's escape, and the manhunt.

"And you think they are hiding in Laramie?"

"At least some of them, but probably not all."

"If they have money, they might be coming my way," she said. "Tell me how I would know they are the ones you want."

Longarm told her the same things that he had told Sheriff Cotton and Earl. "You need to keep a sharp eye out for that cigarette paper and for the money."

71

"I always watch for money, you know that."

"Yeah, I know. That's why I've always wondered why you waste time with a poor federal lawman."

Milly's hand slipped higher until it rested over Longarm's flaccid manhood. "You *know* why I don't think spending time with you is wasted. Or do I have to remind you right now?"

"Stop it." He laughed, feeling himself start to swell. "I'm not up to that tonight and you need to be circulating. The men I seek might well be just passing through. I can't catch them if I'm making love with you."

"What a shame." Milly sighed. "Well, then I had better get to work. There are guests here tonight who have both time and money."

"Look for those Royal Crown cigarettes and let me know what you find."

"I will," Milly promised. "But I can't imagine some rich Englishman riding with a gang of train robbers."

"No," Longarm conceded, "that does not sound very likely, but one never knows. I've seen people I thought to be rich as kings turn out to be thieves. We all put on a little show—even you, Milly."

"Show?" She laughed and brazenly cupped her breasts. "They're not show, Deputy. You of all people know that they're for real—or do you need to be shown all over again right now?"

"Stop it, Milly!" he said in mock anger because he knew that she was simply trying to tease and embarrass him. Milly was actually a very educated and well-read woman, and that was why she of all the women was the only one allowed in the Outpost Hotel to mingle with the rich Eastern guests.

"Bye, honey," Milly said, "I just saw another gold mine come waddling in the door."

"Sure," he said.

Milly, hips swaying provocatively as she crossed the dining room, turned every man's head in the place, even those with wives and girlfriends. Longarm watched with admiration as Milly targeted an older, corpulent man who had all the appearance of wealth.

Longarm shook his head with wonder. Milly had once told him that she had a bank account that was large enough to buy a small cattle ranch or a ten-room whorehouse decked out like a doll cottage. And now, watching Milly ingratiate herself with the rich old man, and seeing the way his nose began to twitch with all the excitement of a bird dog, Longarm was a believer.

Chapter 7

Longarm went to bed that night thinking that he had plenty of baited hooks in the water and wondering which one would land the first fish. It felt wonderful to drop off to sleep in a feather bed with clean sheets and not have to worry about getting rained on in the night or waking up with a stiff back.

He was sleeping like the dead when he was suddenly jarred awake by a loud banging at his door. Longarm reached for his holstered Colt hanging from the headboard.

"Who is it?"

"It's me!"

Longarm relaxed. "Aw, Milly, go away! I'm still asleep."

"Too asleep to talk about an Englishman who smokes Royal Crown cigarettes and has a lot of money to spend on pretty women? Well, if you can find me, we can talk about him sometime. Night, night!"

Longarm blinked rapidly in the darkness. "Wait a minute!" he called, bounding out of the bed and staggering to the door. When he finally got it unlocked, Milly was already descending the stairs to the lobby.

"Milly, dammit, come on back here!"

She turned and looked up at him with a loose smile of amusement. He could see that she was a little tipsy and her hair and lipstick were mussed. Milly had been working and was not in the mood for insults.

"Milly, I'm sorry," Longarm said. "It's just that I've got a lot of sleep to catch up on and I was . . . I was dreaming of you."

"Aw, bullshit! Come on, Longarm, I'll bet you can do better than that!"

Longarm knuckled his eyes. "What time is it?"

Milly shrugged. "Who cares? I guess it will be daylight pretty soon, but I'll manage to be asleep by then and thankfully avoid it."

Longarm yawned. "Would you come on back and talk to me? Otherwise, I'd have to hunt you down and wake you up in a few hours."

"And risk getting shot? That wouldn't be a very smart thing to do, honey."

"Come on," Longarm said, "this is a respectable place. I can't stand out here begging in my almost natural state."

"Say please."

"Please."

"Say that you'll reward me handsomely."

Longarm yawned. "I'll reward you handsomely."

"And scratch my back and kiss me to sleep and—"

"Milly!"

"Oh, all right. I'll settle for the handsome reward," she said, coming back up the stairs and giving Longarm a kiss before she took his hand and led him back into his room.

Milly wasted no time talking, but quickly undressed and climbed into bed with Longarm. She slipped her hand down his flat belly and tickled his privates.

"Come on, Milly!" Longarm said with another yawn. "Don't distract me."

"I *want* to distract you," she said, rolling over to nibble on his earlobe.

"Business before pleasure. Who smokes the Royal Crown cigarettes?"

"Like most men," Milly said peevishly, "your mind is only on one thing. But in your case it's outlaws. Every other man I go to bed with is obsessed with my body."

"Milly," Longarm said, gently pushing her back. "You know how much I enjoy being with you. You're a beautiful and passionate woman."

"Don't stop. Tell me more."

"Dear goddess of love, I need to know about this Englishman who is throwing money around and smoking Royal Crown cigarettes. And I need to know right now because a lot of fine, innocent people were killed and injured on that train."

"All right," Milly said wearily. "I can feel this big scab on your skull and I suspect that you were one of the injured."

"I was," Longarm said, "and I'm lucky to be alive. Now tell me about the man who smokes Royal Crowns."

"I didn't sleep with him tonight. He wanted me to, but I decided to find you first. So you cost me money."

"I'll make it up somehow."

"You darn sure better," Milly said, kissing his cheek. "The man who smokes those funny yellow cigarettes is an associate of the one that you saw me greet when I left your table this evening."

"An associate of that fat old man?"

"Yes. The old man was English and rich. He was also very randy for someone his age. When we were doing it, I thought he was going to burst a . . . well, never mind. Later, we went down for some drinks and I met the young one."

"The man who smokes Royal Crown cigarettes?"

"Yes. He is the old man's nephew and seems to do little more than buy and sell cattle and horses. He talked a lot about traveling on the railroad between Omaha and Sacramento doing business. I gather he also has a stable of thoroughbreds in Reno, Nevada."

"Interesting," Longarm said, "but I doubt that he's a part of that train-robbing gang."

"Why?"

"The man I seek is probably not wealthy. Perhaps comfortable and able to afford a few luxuries like premium cigarettes, but not wealthy."

"But you don't know that."

"That's true." Longarm pulled Milly close. "What is this man's name?"

"Blake Huntington." Milly giggled. "Isn't that a high-sounding hoot? The old rich man I entertained is named Clarence Huntington."

"And where is Blake staying?"

"About four doors down the hall in Room 207," Milly said.

"Are you going to meet him anyplace tomorrow?"

"He invited me to lunch at noon."

"I hope that you accepted."

"I did," Milly replied, starting to sound impatient. "And I can guess where you will be at that hour—turning his room upside down looking for clues."

"That's exactly right. But I won't leave anything that would give away the fact I made a thorough search. I'll be in and out in less than fifteen minutes."

Milly winked. "Don't spend a lot of time. From the way he was looking at me tonight, I expect that we will have a very quick meal and then he'll rush me upstairs in order to get much better acquainted."

"Describe the man."

"Blake is about six feet three, slender, darkly handsome, and he speaks with a slight British accent. He sounds very distinguished. He's well mannered and well dressed. He's a real gentleman, Longarm."

"I'm sure." Longarm curbed his annoyance. "If Blake is such a prize, why don't you try to snag him into marriage?"

"I might just do that except . . ." Milly's voice trailed off and she looked away.

"Except what?"

"I don't know. A professional lady develops a sixth sense about men. She can generally cut through the pretense and look into a man's heart to see if he is honest and kind or unkind."

"And this man is . . . ?"

"Blake Huntington is very unkind," Milly said without hesitation. "There is something very hard and scary about him. And the more Blake tries to cover that something up, the stronger I sense him as being dangerous. That's why I thought you need to investigate this man, because something about him just does not ring true."

"Then don't let him get you alone," Longarm warned.

"Oh, I don't actually think he'd be foolish enough to hurt me. I mean, he must know that it would discredit him with his rich old uncle. And I'll tell you something—Blake is after his uncle's money. He fawns all over that dottering old Englishman. It's really rather sickening."

"This whole thing does not make sense," Longarm said.

"What doesn't make sense?"

"That Blake Huntington could be a train robber. He sounds more like a fortune hunter to me."

Milly pushed herself up so that her exposed breasts were practically hanging in Longarm's face. "Let me tell you something else about Blake before we put each other into a state of bliss."

"I'm listening."

"Blake knows all about that train wreck."

"So?"

"So he was part of it!"

"Nonsense. Milly, he probably just read the papers. I saw the Cheyenne paper down in the lobby. It was all over the front page, and I'm sure that some of the local citizenry have been up there gawking at the wreckage."

"Oh, yeah? Well how many people knew that you were on that train with Eli Wheat?"

"It was no secret."

"And that Wheat escaped?"

"Still no secret."

"Well," Milly said, her lips starting to nibble at Longarm's earlobe again even as her fingers played with his big rod, "Blake Huntington was staying at this hotel during the train wreck. It would have been very easy for him to have joined the robbers and then derailed the train and returned that same evening."

"Yes, that would have been possible. How did you learn that Blake was staying here then?"

"Clarence told me that they had spent four days together out hunting elk in a tent camp just before arriving in Laramie late last week."

"And there can be no mistake about that?"

"No," Milly said, spreading her legs and climbing onto Longarm as she worked his swelling manhood into a stiff pole. "Old Clarence might be out of shape and a little piggish when it comes to satisfying women, but there is nothing wrong with his memory. The top end of that old Englishman is still in fine working order."

Longarm grinned as he felt Milly ease down on his swollen rod. He laced his hands behind his head and watched as she began to work over him in slow, tight circles. The way she moved caused her big breasts to swing enticingly, and when Longarm could stand it no longer he pulled them down to his mouth.

"Oh, yes," Milly said, "with you I can make it, Longarm. With the others, it's just pretending."

"No pretending now," he said, his own hips beginning to move in slick unison to her motion.

Milly was a well-lubricated lovemaking machine. All you had to do was fire her engine. After that, she was capable of running forever. Longarm concentrated on the ceiling, and forced his mind to detach from the building heat in his crotch. Milly liked it to go a long, long time. Maybe even, he thought, glancing out at the window and thinking he saw a hint of light, maybe even until dawn.

"Oh, baby," she purred, "you got what Mama needs!"

Longarm growled, and soon he and Milly were lost in a swirling cloud of passion.

Longarm slept until nine o'clock, then left Milly sleeping and went downstairs for breakfast feeling a little sore in the pants. Milly could do that to a man, and Longarm hoped that he wasn't walking bowlegged. He ate a big breakfast and bought a local newspaper. The *Laramie Gazette* wasn't much of a paper, but what news there was focused on the train wreck. Longarm read every column of print and there wasn't a thing about him and his escaped prisoner, Eli Wheat.

Longarm was on his second cup of coffee when Clarence Huntington, along with a younger man who fit the description of Blake Huntington, strolled into the dining hall and were ushered to a table. Unfortunately, Longarm was not near enough to overhear their conversation, but he could see that both men appeared listless and were probably suffering the aftereffects of a night of drinking and debauchery.

For the next half hour, Longarm watched the pair. When that grew wearisome, he decided to leave. Suddenly Ned Rowe rushed in, out of breath.

"Deputy Long!" he called as he crossed the dining room leaving the odor of manure in his wake. "I found that horse with the broken shoe used in the train wreck!"

Longarm swore in silent fury. Blake Huntington as well as the entire roomful of diners had stopped talking and riveted their attention on the excited blacksmith.

"Yes, sir!" Rowe said, dropping into a chair across from Longarm. "I found that horseshoe, all right!"

"Keep your damned voice down!" Longarm hissed

across the table. "This isn't supposed to be told to the entire town!"

Ned's face fell. "Oh," he said, looking around and realizing that everyone was waiting to hear more. "Well, dammit, how was I supposed to know? Anyway, I found the horse!"

"Let's get out of here," Longarm said, feeling thoroughly disgusted. "We can talk about it outside."

"Talk about it, hell! You can see the horse for yourself!"

Once they were outside, Longarm said, "Show me the horse."

"Sure. Follow me!"

As they hurried down the boardwalk, Longarm tried to assess the damage that might have occurred in the dining room of the Outpost Hotel. If Blake Huntington was a member of the outlaw gang that had derailed the Union Pacific Railroad train and then robbed its mail car safe, he would now be warned and therefore all the more wary. If he was not, then Ned Rowe's excited announcement would have little effect.

"The fella that brought this horse in is a tough-looking hombre, I'll say that. He told me to shoe the horse and that he'd be back for it in an hour."

"In an hour?"

"That's right. But I'm not sure what I'm going to tell him when he returns and his horse isn't shod."

"That won't be your worry," Longarm said. "It'll be mine."

"Well, there the horse is," Ned told him, pointing to a thin roan gelding. "He looks damned hard-used, don't he?"

"He sure does."

Longarm went over and picked up the roan's right front foot. He inspected the broken shoe and said, "This is the horse, all right."

"What are we going to do?"

"Shoe the animal," Longarm said after a moment.

"You mean you're not going to arrest the man?"

"I'd rather follow him awhile and see what he's up to," Longarm said, realizing that he had little choice but to explain. "Most likely, he'll lead me to other members of the gang."

"Yeah!" Ned chuckled. "That sure makes good sense. Maybe we can scoop up the whole bunch!"

"There's no *we* in this," Longarm said. "You just shoe the horse quick and then act natural when its owner returns. I'll follow him."

"But I want to help!"

"Stay out of it!" Longarm snapped. "This isn't your line of work. If there's a capture and reward, I promise it will come to you. But don't mess me up, Ned."

"I know how to take care of myself," Ned told him in an injured voice.

"I'm sure that you do," Longarm said. "But it would just be better if you played your part and left me to handle the rest of it."

Ned didn't act pleased to be excluded, but after more persuasion he agreed to do as Longarm insisted.

"I better get to work," Ned stated. "That fella could be back any time and he's expecting me to be finished with his horse."

"I'll be watching," Longarm promised. "I'll be hiding back in your shop. Everything will turn out just fine."

83

"I hope this one is a murderer and that there is a big reward on his head."

"Yeah," Longarm said, moving into the dim recesses of the blacksmith's shop.

Longarm waited. And waited. And waited. Finally, he struck a match and saw that it was almost noon and that Milly and Blake Huntington would be meeting for lunch.

"Pssst!" Longarm hissed. "Ned!"

The blacksmith had long since finished a hurried shoeing job on the roan, and was once again looking up the street for its owner.

"Pssst! Ned!"

"What?" the blacksmith snapped.

"Come in here for a minute."

Ned took one last look around and marched inside. He was angry and disappointed that the roan's owner had failed to appear as promised. "Deputy, just what the hell do you suppose happened to that guy?"

"I don't know," Longarm said, "but I've got to be somewhere else for the next fifteen or twenty minutes."

"You're leaving?"

"I have to go," Longarm said, realizing that an explanation was warranted but unwilling to offer one to the blacksmith. "If our man returns, stall him awhile. I'll return as soon as I can."

"What if he won't be stalled?"

"Then follow him!"

Ned swore in anger. "You said *you* wanted to follow him alone."

"Look, Ned," Longarm said, "I have to go for a few minutes. I'll be back as soon as I can."

He rushed outside and almost collided with a man.

84

"Deputy Long!" the man shouted, stabbing for his six-gun.

Longarm's own hand made a hurried cross draw for his Colt. He dragged his gun out and fired twice. Then he rolled and fired once more.

The man emptied his gun into the dirt, then pitched forward and was dead before he struck the ground.

"Dammit, that's not what I wanted!" Longarm swore, kneeling beside the dead man and quickly rifling his pockets for clues. All he found was money—about a hundred dollars, which he stuffed in his coat pocket.

"Hey!" Ned Rowe exclaimed. "If you're keeping that fella's money, what in the hell am I going to get out of this?"

"Is this the man we were waiting for?"

"Damn right."

"Then you get the roan horse and saddle," Longarm said, furious with the way things had turned out. "That is, if you keep your mouth shut."

"But what about all that money?"

"It belongs to the Union Pacific."

Longarm reloaded his Colt. He pulled out his pocket watch and noted that it was ten minutes after twelve. There was still time, if Milly kept Blake Huntington occupied over lunch, to search the suspect's room for clues that would link him to the train robbery.

But he had to move fast.

"Hey!" Ned Rowe shouted. "Where are you going? We got a dead man here!"

"I'll be back!" Longarm called, hurrying away before the shots brought a curious crowd.

Chapter 8

"Morning, sir!" the hotel desk clerk sang out as Longarm shot past on his way to the stairs.

"Morning!" Longarm called out as he took the steps two at a time.

He skidded to a halt in the upstairs hallway, and then walked slowly to Blake Huntington's room. First he knocked on the door, and got no answer. Then he tried his own key in the door just in case. When it got him nowhere, he produced a small wire device that had served him well in the past. Sticking it into the door's lock, he took only moments to get the door open. Then he stepped inside, gently closed the door behind him, and moved swiftly to inspect the room.

Longarm was still furious about having to kill the outlaw with the roan horse. If the man had not recognized him and called out his name, things might have worked out fine. But the dead outlaw *had* recognized him, while Longarm could not put a name on the man he'd killed. Even so, he was sure he'd seen the owner of the roan horse someplace.

"Put your mind on the business at hand and stop fuming about what you can't change," Longarm said, forcing himself to concentrate on searching the room.

One thing that was obvious was that, while Blake Huntington might be a gentleman, he was also slovenly. There was a dirty pile of underwear wadded up and pitched in the corner, several empty whiskey bottles on the floor, and an overflowing tray of Royal Crown cigarette butts spilled across his night table.

Longarm went through the dresser first, hunting for some tie-in to the railroad robbery. He found nothing. The top of the dresser was littered with small change, matches, several empty sardine cans, and the tins of other meals quickly consumed.

"One thing for sure," Longarm said. "If he had money, he wouldn't be supping on tinned goods. The man is a fraud."

Longarm searched through the clothes closet, the bathroom, the luggage, and even riffled the pages of several books. He found nothing that would incriminate Blake Huntington or in any way tie him to the train derailment.

"Damn!"

Longarm spied a trash basket filled with more whiskey bottles, a crumpled, week-old newspaper, and some more smelly food tins. Marshal Billy Vail had often preached that a lawman could find more evidence in a trash basket than almost any other place. Longarm carefully went through the contents, and only when he decided there was still nothing of interest and began to stuff everything back did he notice that the Laramie newspaper contained an advertisement for the Union Pacific, with a timetable for the service across the Laramie

Summit to Cheyenne. The advertisement was boldly circled, and beside it were the penciled words "ELI AND DEPUTY."

Longarm's pulse quickened. These three words would not constitute evidence in a court of law, but they told Longarm that, without a shadow of doubt, Blake Huntington was a member of the train-robbing gang. That meant that Huntington was the only real link that Longarm now had with the gang, and that the man would have to be shadowed until more was revealed.

Longarm tore the page out, neatly folded it, and then stuffed it into his pocket. Satisfied that his inspection was complete, Longarm started for the door. Just as his hand clamped onto the knob, he heard the metallic click of a key being inserted in the outside lock.

Longarm whirled and sprang for the window. He tried to open it, but the thing was frozen shut. And even if it had been wide open it would have been a long, long drop to the alley below. He twisted to see the door handle turning, and heard Milly's forced laughter.

Longarm dove for the carpet. He rolled over onto his back, and barely managed to squeeze under the bed just as the door opened.

"Well, now!" the man said in his slightly British accent. "I can see that the hotel needs to get someone up here to do some housekeeping, don't they!"

"I'll say," Milly replied.

There was a moment of silence, and then the bedsprings groaned and sagged to rest against Longarm's chest. He heard the sound of kissing, and then felt the bedsprings moving as the couple began to roll around. Then heavy breathing, and then clothes hitting the floor.

Longarm ground his teeth and cursed himself for not leaving earlier. The last thing he wanted was to be under the bed while this pair coupled.

The bedsprings began to squeak and Longarm could hear Milly start to moan, and he knew from the sound of it that she was faking.

"Oh, baby," the Englishman panted. "What you got is what I want. Roll over."

"No," Milly said quite firmly.

"Aw, come on, beauty! You'll like it!"

"No, I won't! It hurts that way!"

Blake's voice hardened. "Just do it!!"

"No! Blake, stop it!"

Longarm heard fear in Milly's voice. She began to plead and then struggle with the man. The springs pressed down on Longarm as the pair fought, and when Longarm heard the sharp sound of flesh being stuck by flesh, he knew that he could not remain a bystander any longer.

"Please!" Milly cried. "Please stop!"

"You bitch!"

Longarm tore a gash across his chest as he struggled out from under the bed. Blake Huntington was on top of Milly and she was bleeding from the mouth. Longarm jumped up, grabbed the naked man, and hurled him across the room to bounce against the far wall.

Blake Huntington was all man and all mad. Cursing and spitting, he charged Longarm with murder in his eyes. He drove a knee at Longarm's groin that was deflected. But before Longarm could smash Huntington, the man gouged his eye and tried to tear it out of its socket with his thumb.

Longarm struck out powerfully. His knuckles hit bare flesh. Huntington grunted in pain. He backed up, snatched a heavy water pitcher from the dresser, and charged Longarm with every intention of smashing his brains out. Longarm could have drawn his gun and shot the man, but he needed him alive. So he dove for Huntington's ankles. The Englishman's momentum carried him over Longarm and into the window.

The glass shattered and Huntington's scream was hideous, but it ended abruptly when he struck the alley below. Longarm jumped up and ran to the window. Blake Huntington was sprawled on his back, covered with glass and blood. His neck was twisted at a very unnatural angle and he was staring up at Longarm while his naked body twitched.

"Honey!" Milly cried. "He hurt me bad!"

Longarm was also in great pain. The vision in his left eye was blurry. He grabbed Milly's clothes and then pulled her to her feet. Wrapping a blanket around her, Longarm hissed, "Let's get to my room!"

Milly was sobbing, but she understood the sense of urgency. She snatched up an errant shoe and hurried after Longarm toward the door.

"It's too late," he said. The hallway was filled with people who had heard the screaming and yelling.

Longarm took a deep breath. He produced his badge and said in his most officious voice, "Everyone go back to your rooms! I'm United States Deputy Marshal Custis Long and everything is under control!"

He managed to reach his door and get it unlocked. "Get inside and get cleaned up," he told Milly. "I'll be along soon."

"But . . ."

"Just do it!"

He pushed Milly into his room, then slammed the door shut and used his key to lock it. Glaring at the other guests, Longarm repeated, "It's all under control! Now for the last time, get back into your rooms!"

Only one man stood firm—old Clarence Huntington, who had rushed up the stairs. "Where is Blake?"

Before Longarm could stop the man, Huntington barged into Blake's room. His eyes took in the scene, and came to rest on the shattered and bloodstained window.

"No," he whispered.

Longarm jumped into the room behind the man. "I'm a United States deputy marshal and your nephew was beating a woman to death. I tried to stop him and when he attacked, he accidentally tumbled through the window."

Clarence pivoted, and Longarm saw the old man dig into his coat pocket for what was almost sure to be a derringer. Longarm jumped forward. As the derringer came up, Longarm's fist exploded against Clarence's jaw. The old man's eyes crossed and he staggered. He was tough and he was game. Longarm had to hit him twice more: first a brutal uppercut to his protruding belly that lifted Clarence to his toes and turned his face fish-underbelly white, then a left hook that knocked Clarence halfway across the room before he struck the wall and collapsed in a semiconscious heap.

Longarm pressed the flat of his palm against his throbbing eye and walked heavily over to Clarence. "You're under arrest," he said to the old man. "For trying to shoot me and maybe for having something to do with the destruction of railroad property and the murder of innocent passengers."

Clarence Huntington roused himself to mutter something that was not complimentary. Longarm turned to the door. "Someone get me a pitcher of water!"

A moment later, Longarm had water. He poured some into his hand and splashed it into his injured eye. It felt soothing and when he squinted, he could see much better again. Longarm used the remainder of the water to pour over Clarence. The old man sputtered and spit.

"Come on," Longarm said, hauling Clarence to his feet. "You're going to jail."

Clarence stared at Longarm, and when he spoke, his voice was choked with hatred. "I swear that I'll see you in your grave, Deputy!"

"I doubt that," Longarm said. "I doubt that very much."

Clarence, in a fit of renewed vigor, kicked Longarm in the shin, and tried to break free until the lawman drew his Colt. "Keep it up," he said, "and I'll put a bullet in your knee so you can't possibly try and escape."

Clarence started to curse, but when he looked into Longarm's bloodshot eyes, the old Englishman had an abrupt change of heart.

"You'll pay," he said with venom. "You'll pay for everything!"

There was a big crowd in the hallway, and it wasn't easy for Longarm to get Clarence Huntington downstairs, through the lobby, and up the street to the sheriff's office.

"Lock him up, Sheriff!" Longarm ordered, shoving Huntington across the room toward the jail's only cell.

"Mr. Huntington!"

"That's right."

Ike Cotton didn't like this at all. "Mr. Huntington is no criminal!"

"That remains to be seen," Longarm said. "Lock him up on the charge of attempted murder and conspiracy to commit the federal act of railroad destruction."

"You mean . . ."

"Yes," Longarm said, "I mean I think he is part of the gang that derailed the Union Pacific at Laramie Summit."

The sheriff stared at Clarence Huntington and shook his head. "Sir, I want you to know that I don't believe any of those charges. Will you remember that?"

Huntington just stared at him, then turned his hateful gaze back to Longarm. "You murdered my young nephew. I'm not going to stop until you are broken, Deputy. Broken and imprisoned with the kind of men that you have put behind bars. I'll bet that they will know how to punish you far worse than any death by hanging!"

Longarm felt a shiver of apprehension run down his spine, but it never showed. "We'll see," he said. "We'll just see what happens after I search your room."

"You have no right!"

"I have every right," Longarm said.

"I want an attorney!" Huntington screamed. "Sheriff, I demand the best attorney in this town."

"Yes, sir, Mr. Huntington. That'd be Stephen Miller. I'll get him first thing tomorrow."

"Now!"

Sheriff Cotton threw a confused and frightened look at Longarm, and before he could be stopped, the sheriff was bolting out the door and running up the street.

Longarm locked the wealthy man up himself. "I don't know what kind of power you think you have in Laramie, but justice will be served."

"We'll see who wins and who loses," Clarence vowed. "And before my lawyers are through with you, Deputy Long, you'll rue the day that you ever came to Laramie."

"That's big talk. I have evidence that links your nephew to the train derailment."

"What evidence?"

"You'll see when you go to trial," Longarm said. Then he left the sheriff's office and headed back to see if Milly was on the mend.

Chapter 9

Longarm paced back and forth in his room while the doctor examined Milly and a crowd gathered in the street below. It was plain that some of the people were very upset about Longarm being responsible for the deaths of two men in less than an hour, but they were completely ignorant of the facts, so Longarm paid them no mind.

"Well, Doctor?" he asked when the man finally stepped back and appeared to have finished his examination. "Is the prettiest girl in Laramie going to survive?"

"Of course she will," Dr. Wilson said. "Not only survive, but still be pretty."

Longarm's sigh was audible and Milly tried to smile, but winced because her lips were broken. She looked bad now, but Longarm was sure that, in a few weeks, her lips would heal and her facial bruises would disappear.

"Milly," the doctor said, closing his bag, "you're a very lucky woman."

"I don't feel lucky."

95

"You should." Dr. Wilson was a thin, graying man with penetrating blue eyes and a warm smile. "Any one of the blows that you took could have shattered those beautiful cheekbones. I would also have expected a concussion, but even that didn't happen. All you need is a few weeks of rest and recuperation."

"Custis almost got his eye gouged out," Milly said quietly. "I think you'd do better to attend to him."

"He's already looked at my eye," Longarm said. "Just some tiny broken blood vessels. No problem."

The doctor patted Milly on the arm. "I don't know how a man who appeared to be a gentleman like Blake Huntington could use his fists with such savage intent. You're a very fortunate woman."

"I was fortunate that Custis was hiding under the bed and able to save my lovely ass."

The doctor chuckled. "Either way, what you need to do now is get plenty of rest."

"Dr. Wilson," Longarm said, "I understand that Sheriff Ike Cotton has some important questions about the death of Blake Huntington."

"What sort of questions?"

"Beats me. My guess is that Cotton is up for reelection pretty soon and he might be looking to impress folks."

"Impossible," the doctor said with derision. "But as for the victims, there is no question about the cause of death. I examined the bodies of both the man you shot at the livery and Blake Huntington. The shooting victim died of multiple gunshot wounds."

"I'm not concerned about him. There was a witness. It's Blake Huntington's death that mostly seems to be stirring up a hornet's nest."

96

"It shouldn't, and I'll tell the people outside when I leave. If they could see Milly's face, they'd agree that Huntington got exactly what he deserved."

"His Uncle Clarence is determined to nail my hide to the wall over his nephew's death."

"Clarence Huntington was extremely upset when you had him jailed."

"He was out in four hours."

"No matter. His honor had been besmirched. Huntington has some very high-placed friends in Wyoming, and he'll attempt to use them against you, Deputy."

"Who are these friends?"

"Well, one of them happens to be the district circuit judge. Another is no less than the governor."

Longarm scowled. "I've always had a way of getting on the wrong side of powerful people, but I don't see how I could have acted differently. Milly is evidence that Blake Huntington was not what he appeared."

"It was probably not a wise idea to have Clarence jailed," the doctor said, trying hard to be diplomatic.

"Probably not," Longarm agreed. "But he attempted to shoot me. And his nephew was part of the same gang that derailed that train at Laramie Pass."

The doctor frowned. "You've gone on record as stating that, but where is your evidence?"

Longarm had the newspaper page he'd found in the wastebasket but knew that it was insufficient to use in any court of law. "I'd rather not reveal it right now. But something I found tells me Blake was part of that gang."

The doctor walked over to the window and stared down at the street where the angry crowd was milling. "Deputy,

I'm afraid that we've got quite a problem. I'll do whatever I can to calm them down."

"That would be appreciated," Longarm said.

Wilson turned away from the window and it was clear that something was bothering him.

"Speak up," Longarm said. "I can tell that you have something on your mind."

"All right," the doctor said, "You know the law better than I do. So you understand that if it hadn't been for Milly getting so badly beaten, you'd be charged with murder and very likely facing prison, maybe worse."

"Blake Huntington helped to derail that train."

"So you keep saying" the doctor replied, "but he and his rich uncle were also quite popular here. They had plans to invest in Laramie and people looked up to them both. Now you come along, and all of a sudden Blake is dead, and some of the people below see a chance for some big investments flying out the window just like Blake."

"Blake had no money," Longarm said. "I'm sure of that."

"Maybe not, but his uncle did and they were a team." Wilson raised his eyebrows. "I think that our sheriff was very much indebted to them both."

"What are you trying to say?"

"I wouldn't trust Ike Cotton with my back," the doctor said bluntly. "That's what I'm trying to tell you."

"Thanks for the warning." Longarm had already reached the same troubling conclusion.

"Also," the doctor added, "I should warn you that Clarence Huntington has made it public that he is doing everything possible to have you arrested and tried for murder."

"He is?"

"That's right." Doctor Wilson gave Milly some powders for the pain in her head. "You stay in bed, young lady."

"I will," Milly promised, winking at Longarm.

"By yourself!" the doctor ordered sternly.

Milly tried to giggle, but it was too painful. It hurt Longarm to see Milly in pain. He should have acted quicker.

"What's wrong?" she asked.

"The bald truth of the matter is that I've completely messed things up. First I lost Eli Wheat; then I shot one of the gang instead of arresting him and getting a handle on the others; then finally, I couldn't climb out from under a bed fast enough to save you from a beating."

"No one could have known that they were going to derail a train to free Eli Wheat and rob the mail car," Milly argued. "And you *saved* a lot of people that otherwise would have died on that summit."

"Maybe so," Longarm said, knowing it was the truth.

"There is no maybe about that," Dr. Wilson said. "I heard what you did after the train wreck. That's why I know that you would not have thrown Blake Huntington through that window to his death on purpose."

"Thanks," Longarm said.

Doctor Wilson smiled. "Milly, I'll return tomorrow to see how you are feeling."

When they were alone again, Longarm moved back to the window. He did not open the shade, but lifted it slightly and peered down at the angry crowd. He saw the doctor emerge and then begin to try to argue with the crowd, only to be met with a good deal of anger and resistance. Some of it was coming from none other than Sheriff Ike Cotton.

Reaching a decision, Longarm turned back to the room and said, "Milly, you haven't been just kidding me in the past about having money, have you?"

Milly was clearly taken aback by the abrupt question. "I wouldn't kid about that. So why do you ask? Are you thinking about marrying me or something?"

Longarm noted the mirth in her eyes and grinned. "No," he said, "I just wanted to make sure that you are going to be all right."

She reached out and took his hand. "You sound like a man who is about to leave town."

"I've just decided to remove myself from this case," Longarm admitted. "I've done everything wrong."

"No you haven't!"

"Sure I have. I had two members of the gang identified and I killed them both."

"In self-defense! Custis, what else could you have done short of getting yourself shot or brained by a water pitcher?"

"I should have been able to anticipate and capture them alive," Longarm replied. "If I had I'd now have other suspects, and this case might already have been broken open and resulted in the arrest of Eli Wheat and that gang."

"You're much too hard on yourself," Milly said gently.

"Back in Denver, Billy Vail is probably catching hell right now from Clarence Huntington's powerful friends. Billy is not only my boss, but a good friend. This leaves a bad taste in my mouth. I should have handled things better."

Milly took his hand. "Listen," she said gently, "you saved lives on Laramie Summit. Maybe more lives that one night than you've saved over the entire span of your fine career."

"I did what needed doing."

Milly wasn't listening. "And I might have been killed or beaten senseless by Blake if you hadn't been hiding under his bed. You were brave to be there instead of taking off before we arrived."

"You both caught me by surprise," Longarm confessed. "I didn't think you would be coming up so soon."

"Blake wanted me *before* we had lunch. I tried to talk him into waiting but the more I resisted, the angrier and more passionate he became. Finally, there was no choice. I just prayed that you were in and out by the time we arrived. As it turned out, it's a good thing you weren't."

"I'm sorry he broke his damned neck, and I'm at a dead end in this case again, Milly."

Longarm shook his head and continued. "Now I've got to wire Billy and tell him I think it is best that I resign from this case and report back to Denver."

"Do you have to leave right away? I was hoping you could stay with me for a while. If not here in Laramie, then somewhere else."

"I'll ask for a week without pay," Longarm said. "But I can't make any promises."

"And I'm not asking for any." Milly straightened the covers over her and said, "Go on. Send that telegram and then come back and tell me when you get an answer."

Longarm nodded and headed for the telegraph office.

• • •

Longarm received a reply from Billy Vail in less than three hours. It read:

TO HELL WITH CLARENCE HUNTINGTON STOP DERAILMENT AT DONNER PASS CALIFORNIA STOP SEVENTEEN DEAD THIRTY-EIGHT IN-JURED STOP PROCEED WEST AT ONCE STOP CAPTURE NOT KILL FUTURE WITNESSES STOP GOOD HUNTING STOP

Longarm looked up at the telegraph operator. "That's it, huh?"

"That's it, Deputy. Do you think that it's the same gang that derailed our train?"

Longarm studied his telegram. "I can't say for sure, but from the tone of this message, I think that Marshal Vail believes that there might be a connection."

"Donner Pass is what? A thousand miles from here?"

"Close to it. Do you know when the next westbound train passes through Laramie?"

The telegraph operator looked up at a big wall clock with a swinging pendulum. "Next train is coming through in about eight hours."

"Are you sure?" Longarm's luck had been so rotten lately that he found it difficult to believe.

"Would I risk givin' wrong information to someone who fought and killed two tough men in less than an hour?"

Longarm had to grin. "I hope not."

"Damn right I wouldn't."

The telegraph operator, a skinny man in his forties with wire-rimmed glasses and a scraggly beard, spat tobacco juice on the floor and said, "You want me to telegraph your boss and ask for some more travel money?"

"Sure," he said, "why not? I can't be in any more disfavor than I am already."

"Then stop on by before you climb aboard that train," the telegraph operator suggested. "Mr. Vail might even surprise you."

"He can do that," Longarm said on his way out the door.

Longarm returned directly to the Outpost Hotel. The moment he walked into his room and saw Milly, he knew that something was amiss.

"Custis!" she cried in alarm. "They came here wanting to arrest you!"

"Who?"

"Sheriff Cotton! He's got a couple of men and they're looking to put you behind bars."

Longarm didn't wait to figure out the whats or the whys. He was pretty sure that Clarence Huntington must have paid a judge to get an order for his arrest. Whether it was legal or binding meant nothing. Longarm knew that Cotton was just fool enough to try to arrest him and that the more people involved, the more likely people would be killed.

"What are you going to do?" Milly asked.

"If I stay and get arrested, I'm cooked," Longarm decided out loud. "I can't catch Eli Wheat and I can't do my job."

"Then you should go."

"I hate the idea of leaving you alone."

"Who said that I'll be alone?" Milly replied, with a wink of her long eyelashes.

"You'd get a man in here after—"

"No, silly! Not at first anyway. I've got a lot of girl-friends that owe me favors for one thing or another. It might even surprise you to know that I've got some respectable women as close friends."

"Nothing you say or do surprises me," Longarm confessed.

He kissed her cheek and then grabbed his Winchester rifle and bags. "I'll be back again when all this blows over and I've brought the outlaws to justice."

"Don't get caught!" she pleaded. "Now hurry up and go!"

Longarm guessed that he had better scoot. He'd killed two men already in this town, and he sure didn't want to spill the blood of a couple more fools.

Chapter 10

With Ike Cotton and a group of deputies looking to arrest him, Longarm knew that the railroad depot would be covered and that there was no chance of escaping on the train. That meant that he needed to reclaim his horse from Jimmie and leave on the run.

Longarm kept to the alleys most of the way to the livery, hoping to avoid any confrontation. When he saw Jimmie working with a pen of horses, Longarm hurried over to the man.

"Jimmie, I need my sorrel gelding saddled in a hurry."

"You're running from the likes of Sheriff Ike Cotton?" Jimmie asked with surprise.

"I'll be back. But I can't do a damned thing in jail and I don't want to have to gun down the sheriff or any of his fool deputies."

"Where are you going?"

"Better you don't ask."

"Ned Rowe climbed on his horse about an hour ago."

This offhand remark caught Longarm cold. "He left town?"

"That's right. I watched him galloping northwest on his palomino. He sure was in a hurry and he wasn't heading for Cheyenne."

Longarm studied the man. "You're still convinced that Ned is caught up in all this, aren't you?"

"I didn't say that," Jimmie replied. "But nothing that Ned does would surprise me."

Longarm followed Jimmie into the barn and helped him bring out and saddle the sorrel. "Any idea where Ned is going?"

"Nope. But he has a habit of hammering the ends of his horseshoes to a point. You won't have any trouble picking his tracks out. There's a big lightning-shot pine tree about a half mile southwest of here. Ned passed not fifty feet to the north of it and then headed directly toward the north fork of the Laramie River. My hunch is that he's skirting the Union Pacific."

"You think he might be planning to join the gang and help stage another robbery?"

"That possibility has entered my mind." Jimmie toed the dirt. "That fella that you shot, he must have been part of the gang. My thinking is that Ned set him up for you to kill so he could get his share."

"You've got a real suspicious mind," Longarm said. "You should have been a lawman."

"Ain't got the stomach for it. But I do know Ned Rowe. He's no damned good and he's a con man. He figured to let you make a killing for him when he set up that fella with the roan pony."

"But why would Ned leave town now?"

"I dunno," Jimmie said. "I'm just telling you that he did and I figure that, if you overtake him, you'll probably find out a hell of a lot more about that gang."

"Thanks," Longarm said as Jimmie removed the sorrel's halter and replaced it with a bit and bridle. "Jimmie, I just received a telegraph from my boss in Denver saying that there has been another train wreck."

"In Wyoming?"

"No. At Donner Pass. After I catch up with Ned, I'll intercept the railroad and trade in my horse for a train ticket to Donner Pass."

"It would be damned interesting to see if Ned is planning to go thereabouts too, wouldn't it?" Jimmie asked with a lazy smile. " 'Cause you see, if I was a betting man—which I'm not—I'd bet my boots that Ned Rowe is fixin' to do the very same thing you're fixin' to do."

"You don't say?"

"I do say."

Longarm paid the man, tipping him well. "If anyone asks, I rode southeast on my way to Denver."

"Sure thing," Jimmy said, sticking out his hand. "Good luck. If I was a younger man, I'd up and ride after them train-wreckin' bastards."

Longarm mounted his sorrel. "Did you have some friends on that wrecked train?"

The blacksmith's expression turned wintry. "Yeah, I had me a son-in-law that's got both legs broken. The doctor says he'll always walk with a limp and probably never be able to swing up on a horse again. I'm not sure what he's going to do to support my daughter and grandson in the years ahead."

"He could work for you."

"He can if he wants," Jimmie said. "But I'm hard to get

along with, and he favors holding a rope to a blacksmith's hammer."

"He'll learn that blacksmithing is steadier than cowboying and a better life for a family man," Longarm said.

He rode out a few minutes later, careful to keep off the main street. When he had passed beyond the outskirts of town, he put his heels to the sorrel's flanks and headed for the lightning-blackened pine that Jimmy had described. And sure enough, there were the tracks of the horseshoes. Most shoes were squared off at the ends, but for some reason, Ned Rowe forged and hammered them off in points. It was going to make following the blacksmith very easy.

For the next three hours, Longarm pushed the sorrel hard. The trouble was Ned Rowe was in just as much of a hurry. Longarm followed the palomino's tracks, which paralleled the Union Pacific for about twenty miles, than angled due north into some low hills. It was not until sundown that Longarm spotted the glint of metal on the horizon, and guessed that it was the reflection of a concho or even polished spurs or a bit. He was within a mile of overtaking the Laramie blacksmith.

"That will be Ned Rowe," Longarm muttered into the teeth of a cold wind sweeping in from the north.

Longarm followed the tracks for another quarter hour and when he came to a low ridge, he tied his horse to a bush and then went ahead on foot until he reached the crown of the ridge. There he flattened and crawled up to take a peek at the country just beyond.

What he saw was a long, winding valley cut by a meandering stream. Farther out were cottonwoods, a small ranch house with corrals, and some crude outbuildings. And riding up the valley as bold as brass was Ned Rowe on his palomino horse. When the man drew near the house, he drew his side arm and fired it into the air to announce his arrival. With the shot, a pair of men suddenly emerged from the house.

Longarm watched as Rowe dismounted and was enthusiastically greeted. After a few minutes, they all went inside to escape the biting wind.

Longarm eased back from the crown of the ridge and considered his next move. Night was fast falling, and there was an ominous cut to the wind that told Longarm he might be in for another snowstorm or at least a hard rain. The prospect of remaining out on those exposed Wyoming plains was not appealing. For another thing, the three men in the ranch house might be totally innocent of any crime and have nothing to do with the train robbery, despite Jimmie's well-formed suspicions.

Longarm decided to wait another hour. Then it would be dark and he could sneak up on the ranch house and attempt to eavesdrop. If he were detected, he could always try to get the drop on Ned and his friends. He'd then interrogate them until he either had confessions or was convinced that they were innocent.

That decided, Longarm passed the next frigid hour hugging the crown of the ridge. He watched the lights go on in the ranch house and the sun go down in the west. It was a beautiful sunset, but the dark clouds that were momentarily fired by the sunset had the look of rain or snow. One way or another, Longarm decided, he wasn't going to spend the night out on this barren plain and freeze his ass off waiting for something to happen.

When it was time to go, Longarm tightened his cinch and rode down into the valley. It was an excellent site for a cattle ranch and the grass, though brown now, was thick and would be rich feed for cattle and horses next spring.

The ranch house was ablaze with lights, and even though a cold rain began to fall, Longarm had no trouble finding his way to the place, nor did he fear being detected by the three men before he had the drop on them. There was a barn and he rode into it, grateful for the shelter. The sorrel nickered wearily as Longarm unsaddled it and then fed it hay in the middle of the barn floor.

When Longarm left, he pulled the heavy doors shut and hurried across the muddy yard. The ranch house had a front porch, and Longarm stepped lightly onto it drawing his six-gun. He ducked under a front window and listened, hoping to hear something that could make his job easy.

But Ned Rowe and the three men were playing cards and joking among themselves, as near as Longarm could tell over the sound of hard rain falling on the porch's tin roof. When Longarm tried to peek into the window, he discovered that the panes were so filthy both on the inside and outside surfaces that clarity was impossible.

After about fifteen minutes, Longarm realized that he was stiffening from the cold. The wind was icy and he needed to get inside, but he was not ready to barge in the front door because he was almost certain this would result in a bloody gunfight.

Pulling his Stetson low on his forehead, Longarm ducked back under the window, crossed the front porch, and edged along the house until he came to a back door, which he was able to open without a hitch. He drew his gun and stepped into the kitchen, then tiptoed forward until he stopped less than ten feet from the Ned Rowe and his card-playing friends.

"And I'll raise you twenty dollars," Ned challenged.

"Then I'll call you!"

Ned won with three jacks, but Longarm hardly paid the game a moment's thought. What was most interesting was that the three men were betting with a stack of what appeared to be railroad stock certificates. The type that had been stolen during the train wreck.

"Hands up!" Longarm called, stepping into the room with his gun in his fist. "You're all under arrest!"

Ned Rowe's jaw dropped, and he jumped to his feet throwing his hands overhead. But the other pair, not knowing Longarm was a federal marshal and a dead shot, made the mistake of going for their guns.

Longarm's Colt bucked solidly in his fist, and an outlaw crashed over backward with a bullet through his heart. The second man was very fast, and actually cleared leather before Longarm's slug ripped into his shoulder and spun him completely around. The man cried out and his Colt skidded from his grasp.

"Ned," Longarm said, "you want to reach across with your left hand and yank your gun from its holster, then drop it to the floor."

"Jeezus!" Ned choked, trying to smile. "It's *you*! Deputy, I'm sure glad that you came in when you did. I was just about to . . ."

He started to lower his hands, but Longarm yelled, "Keep your mouth shut and your hands high, Ned!"

"What the hell is the matter with you?" Ned cried. "We was just playing cards. And you spooked Fergus and Johnny! You didn't need to shoot them!"

Longarm removed Ned's gun. "Keep your hands over your head and turn around."

"I don't know why you're doing this!" Ned said angrily. "I've tried to help you every bit I can since you came to Laramie. I even figured to get some leads for you out here."

"I'll bet," Longarm said drily.

"Well, I was! These boys are outlaws! I figured that they'd know who was responsible for that train wreck."

"So you just happened to start playing poker using stolen railroad stock certificates as money. Is that it?"

"That's what we were using?" Ned managed a grin. "Hell, Deputy, I didn't know what they was! I swear that I never learned to read."

Longarm didn't believe a word of that. He went over to examine the wounded man, who was writhing around on the floor clasping the his riddled shoulder.

"Settle down," Longarm said, mustering up all the sympathy he felt was warranted for a man who'd tried to shoot him.

"Jeezus but you're a cold-blooded bastard!" Ned exclaimed, staring at the dead man. "You killed Johnny!"

"Better him than me."

Longarm turned his attention back to Fergus. "Here," he said, pulling out a handkerchief and punching it against the wound hard enough to make the outlaw bellow with pain. "Plug it up and hope the bleeding quits before you do."

Fergus accepted the handkerchief. His hand was trembling and his face was white with fear. "Am I lungshot?"

"No."

"Am I going to die?"

112

"Depends," Longarm said.

Fergus stared up at him, waiting. Finally, he blurted out, "Depends on *what*?"

"Depends on if I'm willing to take you to the nearest town and hunt up a doctor."

Fergus pulled the handkerchief away from his wound, and his eyes widened with panic because the handkerchief was already soaked with blood. "I'm bleeding real bad!"

"I want to know who is wrecking and robbing trains," Longarm said, glancing over at Ned. "I want names."

"I don't got any names!" Fergus shouted "I'm a damned horse thief, Marshal! I never robbed a train before!"

"Yeah?" Longarm pulled a cheroot out of his coat pocket and took his time lighting it. He blew smoke in the wounded man's face. "You can say that, but I got a feeling that you're a liar. Who derailed the train at Laramie Summit?"

"I don't know!"

Longarm grabbed Fergus by the shirtfront. "You were playing with stocks taken from that train's safe! Now don't tell me you know nothing! Not if you want help!"

But Fergus stubbornly shook his head back and forth.

"I don't think he knows anything," Ned Rowe said quietly.

Longarm took a deep breath and expelled it slowly. He focused his attention on the Laramie blacksmith. "All right," he said easily. "Let's assume he doesn't know anything. So what do *you* know?"

"Me?"

"Yeah. The game is over, Ned. I want to know the truth. Who's behind the train robberies?"

"I've been helping you!"

Longarm went over to the man. He pressed the barrel of his Colt to Ned's crotch.

"Mister," Longarm said, "I'm cold, hungry, and tired. Furthermore, counting the dead man on the floor, I've killed three men that have crossed me in less than two days. Killing you and letting this self-admitted horse thief bleed to death just doesn't bother me a whole hell of a lot. Give me names!"

"I don't know anything!" Ned pleaded, sweat starting to bead on across his forehead.

"You're a liar, soon to be a eunuch."

"What the hell is that?"

"You know what a gelding is?"

"Sure, but . . ."

Longarm cocked back the hammer of his six-gun. "Figure it out for yourself, Ned."

The man's eyes bugged with terror. "Oh, please!"

"Names, dammit! I need names."

"I didn't do it! I wasn't there and neither was Fergus!"

"Maybe not," Longarm gritted. "But you were helping them somehow. You were in on the train wreck."

Ned licked his lips. "All I did was to shoe some of their horses and . . . and sell 'em some fresh mounts. I didn't know that they were going to send the damn train rolling down a mountainside!"

"I don't believe you," Longarm said. "Say good-bye to women, Ned!"

"All right!" Ned screamed. "I helped them set it up! But neither me nor Fergus ever rode with them. I swear it!"

Longarm had been getting the truth out of men long enough to know when they were too afraid to lie, and Ned was finally telling the truth.

"Names!"

Ned gulped. "Blake Huntington was the brains behind it and you killed him."

"What about his rich Uncle Clarence?"

"The old man didn't know a damn thing about any of it. I'm sure of that much. In secret, Blake hated his uncle. Called him a damned fool and worse."

"More names."

"Big Tom Canyon and a fella they just called Hawk. They was in on it. They're the ones that I helped. The others I saw were just faces. That's all they were, I swear it."

"I've heard of Big Tom Canyon. Who else?"

"There was someone important in Reno. I never heard his name but Blake spoke about him. He has money and he was the one that seemed to be calling the shots."

"What the hell does that mean? Be specific, damn you!"

"He's a politician. They said he was a state senator and that he made his money on the Comstock Lode, but lost most of it a couple years back on mining stocks. All I know is that he was the one that they were counting on to handle things if they went wrong."

"What about Eli Wheat?"

"They talked about helping him escape if he wasn't killed. That's all I know."

Longarm stepped back. There was a train that he still might be able to catch if he was willing to brave this damned storm and ride southwest until he intercepted the Union Pacific. But he'd have to hurry and he'd have to take this pair with him and keep them under arrest until he could find a jail along the rail line. The next one that he knew about wouldn't be until he reached Rock Springs.

"All right," Longarm said, "let's get ready to ride."

"In this weather?" Ned cried. "It's storming out there and the rain will probably turn to snow."

"How far is it to the next Union Pacific depot?"

"Hell, that's clear over at Lookout! It's a good twenty miles or more!"

"Then we'd best stop talking and get to riding," Longarm said, walking over and throwing open the front door. "Help Fergus stand up and let's move!"

As they stepped out into the cold rain drenching the Wyoming prairie, Longarm realized that this was going to be one hell of a tough night.

Chapter 11

Longarm barely remembered the little combination depot and coal and water station at Lookout. If he was in luck, he would find a competent telegraph operator who could relay a message back to Billy Vail about the vital information he'd just gained from his captives.

Longarm had to prod his prisoners hard to get their horses ready to leave the ranch. The wounded man named Fergus was especially difficult and argumentative.

"I'll probably bleed to death in the saddle before we reach that train!" he wailed.

"You'll bleed to death for sure if you don't climb into that saddle and quit talking," Longarm warned. "Because I'll shoot you again."

Ned Rowe was more cooperative. He decided that Longarm had bought his story, and now was trying hard to be cooperative. Longarm saw little reason to change the man's false impression of things and risk turning cooperation into desperation.

"Damn, it's cold!" Ned exclaimed, tightening his cinch.

"Quit jawin' and mount up," Longarm said.

117

"I sure wish that we could at least wait until tomorrow morning," Ned groused. "We could freeze to death before we reach shelter."

"That's a chance we'll just have to take." Longarm snapped, watching the heavy rain sheet off the roof to cascade across the barn's open doorway like a waterfall.

"I can't get on my horse!" Fergus choked. "Not with this bad shoulder."

Longarm watched the man struggle. Each time Fergus started to lift his leg over his cantle, he lost his balance and fell back.

"All right," Longarm said, starting to go over to help the man.

He was still on his way over when Fergus made his move. "Yaw!" he shouted, leaping into the saddle and booting his horse through the barn door and out into the heavy rain. In less than two seconds, the man had vanished.

"Damn!" Longarm swore. He mounted his horse. "Dismount!"

"What?" Ned cried.

"I said dismount!"

Ned dismounted, and Longarm grabbed his horse's reins.

"Hey!" Ned shouted. "Are you leavin' me?"

"I'll be right back," Longarm yelled. "And you'd better be here."

Longarm shot out of the barn dragging Ned's saddled horse. He was furious at the wounded man for making a run for it in such bad weather. Before he'd galloped across the yard, the rain had soaked him to the bone. It took him no more than three or four minutes to overtake Fergus, who was bent over his saddle horn and riding for his life.

When the wounded man saw Longarm overtaking him, he cursed and tried to urge his horse into a gully running strong with rainwater, but the animal skidded to an abrupt halt and Fergus lost his seat. The wounded outlaw spilled headfirst into the gully and rolled down into the muddy torrent.

"Come on, get out of there before you drown, you damned fool!" Longarm ordered.

"No! You have to shoot me again, you big bastard! I ain't going to hang for that train wreck!"

"That's up to a judge!" Longarm yelled. "But if you want to save the taxpayers some money, then I *will* shoot you!"

Longarm drew his Colt, took aim, and fired. His bullet ripped away Fergus's empty holster and the man yelped in fear, then came scrambling out of the gully like it was crawling with rattlesnakes.

"Get on your horse!" Longarm ordered.

"I can't! Remember?"

Longarm was wet, chilled, and miserable. He used a second bullet, which sent Fergus's Stetson flying back into the gully. "I won't be suckered a second time," he warned.

Fergus found a way to mount his horse. Longarm led him and the other spare horse back through the driving rain to the barn.

"All right, Ned! Come on out of there and let's ride!"

No answer.

Longarm drew his six-gun again and dismounted. He expected that Ned might be waiting to ambush him with a pitchfork or a hay hook. But Longarm was mistaken

119

because, after a few frantic moments of searching, it was clear that Ned Rowe had escaped into the stormy night.

Longarm was fit to be tied. He now realized that, in his rush to overtake Fergus, Longarm had forgotten that there was a third horse belonging to the man he'd killed. And it was this horse that Ned had used to bolt for freedom.

"Dammit!" Longarm swore, slogging through the mud searching for Ned's tracks.

But the rain was coming down too hard and there was no telling in which direction Ned had chosen to run.

"He got clean away, didn't he?" Fergus said with a twisted and triumphant leer.

"Yeah, he did," Longarm replied. "I haven't got time to hunt him down tonight, but I'll find him later. Just like I'll track down Eli Wheat."

"You might not be so lucky a second time with Eli," Fergus said as Longarm remounted. "You go lookin' for them boys, they'll kill you, and I hope to hell I'm there to watch you die."

"You won't be," Longarm promised, for he had already decided to turn his prisoners over to the sheriff in Rock Springs, who was a man that could be trusted. "Let's ride!"

If anything, the rain came down harder as they rode through that awful night in the direction of the station at Lookout. A few hours before dawn, rain turned to sleet. A faint gray dawn hugged the eastern horizon and showed Longarm the railroad tracks.

"Let's go!" he urged, reining west.

"Lookout is back toward Laramie," Fergus argued. "We missed it by riding too far west."

"Then what's the next depot?"

"There ain't nothing left at what used to be the Miser depot. So the next depot is Rock Creek. But that's another seven or eight miles!"

"Then we'd better put the spurs to these ponies," Longarm said, booting his tired sorrel into a gallop across the sloppy ground that paralleled the tracks.

The westbound train overtook them before they could make it all the way to Rock Creek. Longarm heard its eerie whistle blow, and reined his horse up to see the locomotive lumber toward them in the distance. The ground was rising toward Rock Creek and the train was moving slow, its stack spewing smoke into the sleet.

"What are you gonna do now?" the wounded man crowed. "We lost the damned race."

Longarm knew that there really was only one thing that he could do and that was to stop the train. "Let's ride up on those tracks."

"What?"

"I said come on!" Longarm ordered, dragging along the horses and scrambling up on the roadbed.

"That train won't stop!" Fergus shouted with rising panic in his voice. "It'll think we're train robbers and it'll run us the hell down!"

"No one lives forever," Longarm replied, dismounting and hauling Fergus out of the saddle. He ripped the man to his knees, drew his six-gun, and said, "Lay down across the rails."

"What?"

"Lay down!"

Fergus lay down on the wet tracks. He was at the end of his rope, hurt, confused, and weakened by loss of blood, his mental and physical reserves gone.

"You gonna let him run me over!" Fergus screamed as the train moved inexorably closer. It was close enough already that the tracks were shaking and the horses were snorting nervously.

"I want more names!" Longarm called over the sound of the approaching train. "I want *all* the names or this train is going to cut you into three messy pieces!"

"Oh, Lord!" Fergus howled, his eyes wild. "First you shoot me, now this!"

"Names!"

With one eye on the looming locomotive and another on Longarm, Fergus spat out the names like bullets from the muzzle of a Gatling gun. "Big Tom Canyon. Hawk Jenkins. Two-Fingered Earl. Shorty Hamilton. Bob Orr. Indian Red Lopez! That's all I know. Please, don't do this!"

Longarm planted his boot firmly on the back of Fergus's neck and turned the horses loose to run a short ways off, where they stood heads down and rumps to the driving sleet.

Longarm raised his hand in the frontier signal of peace and said to his prisoner, "Well, Fergus, we'll just let the engineer decide your fate."

Fergus howled and screeched like crazy until the train began to slow. If it hadn't, Longarm would have let the man up, and then he'd have jumped on board and forced the engineer to stop.

The engineer looked frightened, and there was a rifle in both his and the fireman's fist when the big locomotive ground to a shuddering halt.

"What the hell is going on down there?" the engineer called out.

"I'm a federal officer of the law. I got a prisoner and a big need to get to Reno."

"This ain't no damned way to board a train!"

Longarm ignored the outburst. "Here's my badge!" he said, digging it out of his pocket to display to the two nervous railroad men. "Can we load our horses?"

"Hell, no!"

Longarm shook his head. He looked to the young fireman and said, "If my prisoner moves, you have my permission to shoot him again."

The fireman was barely out of his teens, a tall, powerful young man covered with the wet muck and grime of coal dust. Only his teeth and eyes showed white when he said, "You mean he's already been shot?"

"That's exactly what I mean. And I'll shoot *you* if you let him run away in this storm!"

The fireman raised his rifle, took aim on Fergus's chest, and said. "You're coyote bait if you move, mister."

Longarm hurried over to the horses and quickly removed their saddles, blankets, and bridles. He carried his own saddle, Winchester, bedroll, and canvas bag with provisions to the train, where a conductor helped him and his wounded prisoner climb on board.

"United States Marshal Deputy Long," Longarm announced to the handful of startled passengers, most of whom had been sound asleep when the train had jarred them awake during its sudden and unscheduled stop. "And this here is my prisoner, and don't go feeling sorry for the bastard because he's part of the same bunch that wrecked the train at Laramie Summit."

The passengers appeared to be shocked by this announcement. Or maybe it was Fergus's deathly pallor that shocked them as well, because the wounded outlaw was trembling with cold and fear.

"Is he going to die?" an old lady asked.

"I doubt it," Longarm said.

"If he does, it would serve him right for his role in killing so many innocent people up there on the summit."

"I couldn't agree with you more."

It was only after the train was rolling along slowly again that a tall, lean cowboy with missing front teeth whistled, "What about them horses that you turned loose?"

"What about them?"

"Well, you comin' back for 'em?"

"Not likely."

A moment's silence, then he said, "Three good saddle horses and two saddles is worth at least two, maybe three months' cowboyin' wages."

"You might not even catch them," Longarm said, reading the cowboy's intent. "And this train has already gone at least a mile."

"I don't mind the walk, sir. I'd walk back to Laramie for the value of them horses and saddles."

For some reason, Longarm felt compelled to make one final argument. "My friend, it's freezing out there and not only might you get stranded, but you also might catch your death of pneumonia."

But the cowboy was already up and moving down the aisle. "I'd like to take my own chances, if you don't mind. That sorrel horse was a damned fine-looking animal."

"He was as good as his looks," Longarm replied. "And if you can find him in this storm, then he's yours with the

American taxpayers' blessings."

"Well, thank you, America!"

And with that, the cowboy dashed out of the coach and disappeared into the driving sleet.

Chapter 12

Longarm put Fergus up against the window and took the aisle seat. He was bitterly cold and wet. At the rear of the coach, a middle-aged and very undistinguished-looking couple held a quick whispered conversation. Moments later, the couple came forward to stand beside Longarm.

"We want to trade seats with you," the man announced. "You're cold and wet and our seats are close beside the stove."

Longarm looked up at the man. He thought that he should decline the generous offer, but his teeth were chattering and he knew that would be foolish.

"We're much obliged," he said. "But I must warn you that our seats are going to be damp and . . ."

"Never mind that," the woman said with a warm smile. "We've some blankets we can spread over them."

"You're very kind."

"We are the Friedlanders." The couple were like a pair of sweet-faced marionettes. They bowed slightly in unison as the woman said, "My name is Ida and this is my husband, Luke. We are originally from Kentucky."

Longarm removed his hat. He knew that he must look a fright. He smiled. "Kentucky is the flower of the South. And you are fine people to be so charitable."

"We respect the law and have no wish to see anyone suffer needlessly," Ida said. She smiled, and her blue eyes flicked to Fergus and then returned to Longarm. "Which brings us to another matter."

"And that would be?"

"My father was a surgeon in the Confederate Army. I traveled with him and . . . well, it was a terrible thing for a child to see, but I learned a great deal about bullet, shrapnel, and saber wounds. In the years we have been together, my husband and I have patched up many a brave man."

"There is nothing particularly brave about either myself or this prisoner," Longarm said, "but seeing as how I doubt we'll find a surgeon until we reach Rock Springs, if then, you're welcome to have a look at his bullet wound."

But Fergus recoiled. "You're mighty kind, ma'am, but I don't want no woman diggin' around in my shoulder. I'd just as soon wait for a real doctor."

"That would be a mistake," Ida said. "I can tell by your color that you are about to go into shock. Probably the cold has something to do with it, but so does blood loss. Furthermore, a bullet should never remain buried in flesh. It quickly causes corruption and blood poisoning."

"My wife knows what she is talking about," Luke said quietly. "Ida has more experience than most any surgeon that you'd be lucky enough to find this side of Reno. And she always carries her father's surgical instruments—just in case we have the opportunity to help save a life."

"I damn sure do want to live long enough to see Deputy Long get shot," Fergus snarled.

"Then you'd better let Ida dig out that bullet," Longarm said. "It doesn't matter one way or the other to me. You already gave me the names of the members of the gang when you thought I was going to let the train run you over. I was bluffing, of course, but it worked just like I'd expected."

"You bastard!"

Longarm balled his fist, but Ida Friedlander objected. "This man may be a murderer, but he is still a human being made in the image of God."

"If so," Longarm said, "the Father's image is tarnished beyond recognition."

"Please let us take him into a car where we can examine him and remove the bullet if that is possible."

"All right," Longarm agreed, "but I'm coming along and I won't take my eyes off him for even a minute. Fergus may look like a whipped dog, but he's as cunning as a fox and as ruthless as a wolverine."

"He is a human being," Luke said. "We may hate the sin but not the sinner."

Longarm wasn't sure that he agreed. Furthermore, this new development was annoying. A few minutes before he thought that he'd be spending time beside the stove to thaw out his bones. Now, he was going to have to search out some cold baggage or mail car and stand guard while these two Good Samaritans tried to save the wounded outlaw's worthless life.

"Let's get this over with," Longarm said after a long, uneasy silence. "But Ida, if my prisoner does not survive the operation, I want you to know that you will not greatly disappoint me or any of the passengers fortunate enough to survive the Laramie Summit train wreck."

Ida gave him a look that said she felt pity for a man so unforgiving as Longarm. With her husband in the lead, she walked down the aisle, and then was followed by Fergus, while Longarm marched along behind.

They had to go all the way back to the mail car before they could find a place to examine Fergus.

"Take off your coat and your shirt, please," Ida requested with a smile of encouragement.

"I'll freeze to death!"

Luke moved over to the small stove and addressed the frightened mail clerk. "Do you suppose we can stoke up the fire and get some warmth in here?"

The clerk, a thin, ascetic-looking fellow, bobbed his pointed chin like a bird. His voice was high-pitched and carping when he complained, "They don't give me enough coal to burn. Not near enough! I really freeze in this weather, and I'm trying to ration it out to last until this train makes Rock Springs."

Longarm went over to the coal bin and, sure enough, there was not more than a few shovelfuls. It might get the car warm enough so that you could not see your own breath, but not much warmer. "This is all the coal you have?"

"That's right!" the clerk complained wearily. "It's awful, isn't it?"

"I'll get you more coal at the next stop," Longarm promised as he took the shovel and emptied the bin into the stove. "But right now, we've got to have some heat. I'm about to freeze to death myself."

129

They waited a few minutes for the stove to warm up the mail car, and then Fergus gritted his teeth and worked himself out of his coat and shirt.

"Please sit down," Ida requested. "I'm a head shorter than you, young man. I can't begin to examine your wound standing on my tiptoes."

Fergus took a seat. He was shivering violently despite the newfound warmth of the crackling stove. His shoulder wound was a mess. There was just no other way for Longarm to describe the damage caused by his bullet.

"What do you think?" Fergus asked nervously. "It's pretty bad, huh?"

"It looks worse than it is," Ida said, shifting around the chair to probe around the area of Fergus's shoulder blade. "I think the bullet is very near the blade bone. I believe that it can easily be removed."

"Are you sure?" Fergus asked, looking very nervous.

"No one can be exactly sure," Ida said. "But that's my opinion." She motioned to Luke. The man nodded his head and hurriedly left the mail car.

"Where's he going?" Fergus asked in a thin, reedy voice.

"To get my father's medical bags. We have a bottle of chloroform."

Fergus gulped several times. He even looked to Longarm with a plea in his eyes and said, "You think that I ought to let her do this, Deputy?"

"It's a long way to Reno, the first place where we're likely to find a real surgeon. If it was me, I'd give Mrs. Friedlander the benefit of the doubt."

"I don't know about that there chloryform stuff she's talking about. I'd rather have some whiskey."

"Too bad," Longarm said. "That's not possible."

"The chloroform is better," Ida said. "You won't feel as bad afterward. It's a little more difficult to administer the precise dosage necessary, but I've done it many times before and I'm absolutely convinced that I will not put you to sleep permanently."

"Well, good!"

Ida smiled. "I should tell you that there is already suppuration leaking from the wound. It doesn't smell good, but I've some medicines that will fight the gangrene. I would not do this operation if I did not feel confident that your life can yet be saved."

Fergus wrapped his arms around his bony torso and hugged himself to keep from shaking. He looked as white as snow, very thin and very worried. "I just don't know what to do!" he whined.

"Do what the lady says," Longarm advised, sure that he could also smell the gangrenous rot.

Maybe Fergus could smell it too, because he chewed his lower lip for a few seconds and then finally nodded his head. "All right, let's get this over with. But I want *whiskey*, not that chloryform stuff!"

Longarm was about to tell Fergus that it didn't matter what he wanted, that whiskey was out of the question unless perhaps as a farewell drink.

But Ida said, "I have some whiskey in the medical bag. It's a good painkiller as well as disinfectant. You can have the whole bottle."

Fergus brightened considerably at this news. "Now you're talking!"

A few minutes later, Fergus was guzzling whiskey and Ida was spreading out her father's medical kit. She neatly arranged the shiny surgical instruments on the mail car worktable. When everything was in readiness, she said, "I think we had better get started, Mr. Fergus."

The outlaw showed no interest in relinquishing the bottle of whiskey, which he had already half emptied. He eased back on the table, and his eyes burned with hatred when he stared at Longarm. Then, turning back to Ida Friedlander, he said, "All right, let's get the damn bullet out."

"Roll over on your stomach."

Fergus rolled over and pushed himself up on his elbows so that he could pour whiskey down his gullet. When he finished the bottle, he dropped it on the floor. It rolled up against the wall and Fergus hissed, "Let's go!"

Longarm watched closely as Ida took a scalpel from her husband. She made a quick, deep incision that lifted Fergus howling off the table. Then he gripped the edge of the table and ground his teeth.

Ida Friedlander proved herself to be a skilled surgeon. She was into the wound in seconds, and her husband kept feeding her forceps to clamp off the worst bleeding. She quickly dug Longarm's misshapen bullet out, and packed the wound with disinfectant powder before suturing the incision.

The entire operation took less than twenty minutes. When it was over, Ida heaved an obvious sigh of relief and said, "Mr. Fergus, how are you?"

"I've been better," he whispered. "Help me sit up."

"It would be good for you to keep lying down."

"I want to sit up, damn you!"

Longarm stepped forward. He grabbed Fergus by the hair and yanked his head off the table. "Don't you dare talk like that to a woman who probably saved your life!"

"It's all right," Ida said. "Please let him go."

Longarm released the man's hair. Fergus's jaw bounced on the table, and then the man pushed himself into a sitting position.

For a moment, all eyes were on Longarm, who was clearly struggling with his anger. And in that moment, Fergus happened to glance down and see the bloody surgical instruments. Without warning, his right hand grabbed the scalpel and his left hand fisted Ida's hair.

Before Longarm could move, the scalpel was pressed to Ida's throat. Luke make a tortured sound in his throat. He took a step forward and cried, "Please don't kill her!"

Fergus was woozy from blood loss and whiskey. He licked his lips and his eyes radiated hatred as he stared at Longarm. "You pull that big gun of yours and try to shoot me again," he choked, "and this lady is a dead Samaritan! You understand me?"

"I understand you perfectly."

Fergus giggled. "No surgeon in the world is fast enough to keep this woman from bleeding to death once I cut her throat from ear to ear."

"You'd do that after what Mrs. Friedlander did to save your worthless life?"

"Deputy, I'll kill her in a heartbeat if that's what it takes! Now, with your left hand, ease that gun out of your holster."

Longarm was still shaking; only it was no longer from the cold—it was with fury. He knew without a doubt that once Fergus had his gun, the man would shoot him and the rest of them to death. Handing Fergus a loaded six-gun was not even a remote consideration.

"You should think this out again," Longarm warned. "It's the whiskey that's made you crazy."

"Oh, no!" Fergus cried. "It's the fact that I was at Laramie Summit and so was Ned Rowe. You'd have gotten someone to squeal and say that sooner or later, and I'd have been sentenced to hang. That's why I'm getting out of here now!"

Fergus motioned to the large sliding door. "Tell the clerk to open it wide."

"Open it," Longarm said, not daring to move.

The clerk rushed over to the door, threw the latch, and pushed the door open. All the heat that had been generated by the fire was lost as cold air blasted into the mail car. Mail still unsorted and resting in trays took flight in a blizzard of paper that swirled in the air. Outside, the rain was still falling and the higher sage-covered hills were dusted with a blanket of glistening snow.

"Give me your gun," Fergus repeated. "Hand it over *now*!"

"And then what?"

Fergus actually giggled. "Then you're going to jump off the train. If you're lucky, you'll live. If not, well, no one lives forever."

"And the others?"

"I'll lock them in this room and they won't be harmed."

"Don't believe him!" Luke cried. "In my heart I now understand that this man is a killer! He is possessed by Satan!"

Longarm pretended to disagree. "He'll keep his word because there is no reason to kill you folks."

"But a man possessed by the Devil needs no reason!"

"Shut up!" Fergus cried. "Old man, you shut up or I'll slit your woman's throat!"

A trickle of blood seeped down Ida's throat and stained her collar. But Ida Friedlander was a marvel of control. She didn't even whimper.

"For the last time, give me your gun!" Fergus shrieked.

Longarm slowly extracted his gun and laid it on the table. His mind was spinning like the wheels of a slot machine, but there was no hope of a payoff.

"Push the gun over here!"

Longarm nodded, and his free hand brushed his vest, thumb hooking into his watch chain. To everyone in the mail car it appeared as a thoughtless move, but as Fergus reached for the six-gun, Longarm's hand dug into his vest pocket and instead of a watch fob, out came his solid-brass twin-barreled .44-caliber derringer.

Ida bit Fergus's wrist. The scalpel clattered on the table and Ida threw herself over backward, spilling across the floor. Luke jumped to cover her body with his own.

Fergus lunged for the Colt resting only inches from his grasp. His fingers closed on the big weapon as the derringer in Longarm's fist bucked solidly and a blue hole appeared just over Fergus's right eye. Fergus's eyes rolled upward as a dribble of blood crested the bridge of his nose and splashed to the table. Fergus's fingers drummed on the table and then quivered.

Chapter 13

"Dammit anyway!" Longarm swore. "Why'd Fergus have to go and do a fool thing like that for?"

Longarm peered closely at the woman who had almost had her neck slit open. "Are you all right, Ida?"

"Why . . . I think so."

Luke helped his wife to her feet. There was a smear of blood on her throat, but it was clearly just a superficial wound. Ida was visibly shaken, but then, Longarm knew that anyone would have been upset after such a harrowing ordeal.

"Ida, honey?"

"I'm all right, Luke," she whispered as her husband pulled a clean handkerchief out of his back pocket and pressed it to the scalpel cut at her neck.

"I'm going to take her back to the coach," Luke said after Ida appeared to regain her composure.

"Good idea," Longarm said in agreement.

"What about the body?" the mail clerk demanded when the couple had exited the mail car. "Deputy, you ain't just going to leave it lying there on the floor with him staring up at the ceiling. Are you?"

"What do you want me to do?" Longarm asked with rising annoyance. "Kick Fergus out the door and feed the coyotes and the buzzards?"

"Well, no, sir! But you can't just leave him lying there staring that way!"

"The hell I can't," Longarm said, pulling the sliding door shut and slamming the latch down hard. "I imagine that you have a lot of work to do. So do it!"

Longarm left the mail car for another coach, seeking warmth and whiskey and maybe even a pretty woman to remind him that there was still beauty in the world.

He found two of the three fairly quickly.

"Excuse me, miss, but would you mind if I sat down here close to the stove? I'm so cold that I'm about to shake my teeth out."

The woman turned and stared at Longarm with unconcealed apprehension. She was obviously taken aback by his rough, unshaven, and unwashed appearance.

"Miss, my name is Custis Long. I'm a federal officer of the law."

Longarm reached into his pocket, rummaged around for a moment, and brought out his badge. "See?"

"Yes, I see," she said, finding her tongue and relaxing. "And you do look damp and very cold."

"I'm the fella that stopped this train a while back," Longarm explained, easing into the seat beside her.

"But where is your prisoner?"

"Well, ma'am, he died real suddenly of poisoning."

"Poisoning?"

"Yep. Took us all by surprise."

"How terrible!" The woman leaned forward and studied him intently. "Was it something he ate or drank?"

"I would rather not talk about it, if you don't mind."

"I'm sorry. My name is Veronica Greenwald. I'm a schoolteacher and I'm on my way to Reno. I've accepted a teaching position there."

"Reno is a nice town."

"Have you been there often?"

"Four or five times. I'm on my way there now, as a matter of fact."

"How nice."

The woman smiled and Longarm felt warmed inside. Veronica appeared to be in her early thirties. She wore wire-rimmed glasses, and her blond hair was pulled back into a severe bun. Even so, she was very pretty. She had classic features, and her starched white blouse could not hide the fact that she was exceedingly well endowed.

"I suppose," Veronica said, "that you'll have all kinds of reports and things to write concerning the death of your prisoner."

"I suppose."

"Was he . . . was he really awful?"

"He was a liar, a horse thief, and a murderer." Longarm said flatly. "He tried to cut a lady's throat after she saved his worthless life."

"Oh, dear!" Veronica looked away. "I know that there are men that evil, but I've never met one."

"Consider yourself very lucky," Longarm said with conviction. "Where are you from?"

"Iowa. I was raised on a farm. I was raised by a farmer and fell in love with a boy who became a farmer."

"You're married?"

"No, Mr. Long. Three months ago a tornado came through our little town and killed my fiancé. It wiped out our family farm and flattened our school, church, and most of Grover City's main street."

"I'm sorry."

"It was a disaster. I decided to go West and try to start over again. It was too painful to remain in Grover City. Fortunately, I was able to secure the promise of employment in Reno. I understand that the person I replace has contracted some sort of very serious illness and must forsake the classroom at once."

"I see."

They chatted for a few more moments, then lapsed into a comfortable silence. Longarm briskly rubbed his hands together trying to warm them. He leaned his head back against the seat cushion feeling angry and even a little depressed for having lost another prisoner. Fergus was the fourth man he'd killed while on this case; only Ned Rowe, of the gang members he'd encountered, had escaped with his life.

"I think," Veronica observed after about an hour, "that the storm is passing on."

Longarm gazed out the window and then at Veronica. "There is no doubt that the sun is going to shine again."

"That's an odd way of putting it."

"I just meant that your eyes are as blue and lovely as a summer sky and your smile is warmer than any sunlight."

Veronica blushed. "My, you *are* a flatterer!"

"I'm an honest man."

"Not entirely."

"What does that mean?"

"It means that just before you came, the conductor

passed through saying that an outlaw had been shot by a deputy in the mail car."

"I see. Then why, Miss Greenwald, did you pretend not to know?"

"I'm sorry. I wanted to hear you tell me what happened." Veronica smiled. "Really, Mr. Long, why did you tell me that the prisoner was poisoned?"

"Because he was! He died of a very sudden and severe case of lead poisoning."

It wasn't meant as a joke, and Veronica did not laugh or even smile. She just blinked, her eyes large and luminous behind her glasses as she regarded her companion for a moment and then turned to stare out the window.

At Rock Springs, Longarm sent Billy Vail another telegram:

EN ROUTE TO RENO STOP NED ROWE ESCAPED NEAR LARAMIE STOP OTHER PRISONERS ALL CONTRACTED FATAL DOSE OF LEAD POISONING STOP REPLY TO RENO AT ONCE STOP

"A fatal dose of lead poisoning?" the telegraph operator asked with raised eyebrows.

"Just send the message, okay?"

"Sure thing."

Once his telegram had been sent, Longarm hurried outside. He considered visiting the sheriff, who was his friend, but when he passed by the man's office, it was locked and empty.

Longarm was amazed at how Rock Springs was growing. The streets were filled with wagons and pedestrians. And while there were some ranches and farms in the neighborhood, as evidenced by a handful of cowboys, Rock Springs was unquestionably a railroad town. Its coal mines, owned by the Union Pacific, were among the largest west of the Mississippi River and of vital importance to keeping the railroad moving. Because of the prominence of coal mining, there were huge open-pit mines nearby and dozens of spur tracks leading off to those gaping pits.

Like Laramie and Cheyenne, Rock Springs could boast a colorful past. In 1861, a Pony Express rider, detouring to escape marauding Indians, had discovered the sweet-water springs flowing out of a massive rock formation. This had given Rock Springs its name. Later, the site became a stage station, and when the Union Pacific arrived, the town had already mushroomed into one of the largest in the territory, and boasted a growing population and evidence of continuing prosperity.

About ten years earlier, a significant Chinese population had been recruited to Rock Springs by its mine owners in order to defeat a miners' strike. Longarm recalled that a mob of whites had soon attacked and pillaged the thriving Chinatown and set it on fire. The leaders of the mob had put a twenty-dollar bounty on every Chinaman, and six hundred dollars had been claimed before the Governor of Wyoming had sent federal troops in to stop further loss of life among the terrified Chinese. Now, as Longarm hurried up K Street, he could see that Chinatown had been rebuilt larger than ever.

"I want a bath and a shave," Longarm told the Chinaman in the barbershop.

The man bowed and hurried away, his long, braided queue bobbing like a cork on a fishing line. In minutes, Longarm was soaking in a copper tub while the Chinaman washed, dried, and pressed his clothes, then poured Longarm a cup of delicious herb tea and waited to give him the finest shave of his life.

Two hours later and only a dollar shorter, Longarm returned to board the train. He caught his reflection in the train windows, and was satisfied that he was looking almost human again.

Veronica barely recognized Longarm when he took his seat. "What a difference two hours can make!" she exclaimed. "How could you get so much done in such a short time?"

"The Chinese are amazing people," Longarm explained. "They can do miracles and are extremely quick and efficient."

Veronica smiled. "I have to admit that I didn't realize how handsome a man you are, Custis."

"I hope that we have a chance to become better acquainted in Reno."

"I doubt that will be possible."

"Oh?"

"You told me that there was another train wreck at Donner Pass. I'm sure that every bit of your time and energy will be directed toward that terrible crime."

"Well, it will," he said quickly. "But these things don't usually take forever to clear up. I was thinking about afterward."

"Afterward what?"

Longarm took Veronica's hand. "Afterward we might go for a long buggy ride and then have dinner."

"That would be lovely . . . if it's all that you have in mind."

He decided to act mildly offended. "Why, Miss Greenwald! Whatever are you trying to say?"

"I'm trying to say that when you fell asleep this afternoon you had what appeared to be a very . . . stimulating dream."

"I did?"

"Yes. Very! You were calling a woman by name."

"I was?" Longarm could feel his cheeks warming.

"A Miss Martha Noble . . . at first."

Longarm gulped. "You mean there were others?"

"Oh, yes! Surely the name of a woman named Milly is enough to quicken your desire, eh, Mr. Long?"

Longarm sighed. There was really nothing he could say, so he excused himself and went for a short walk and to smoke a cheroot. Maybe by the time they arrived in Reno, Miss Greenwald would be inclined to forget about his amorous past.

Chapter 14

When the train finally pulled into Reno, a federal marshal was standing in the depot waiting for Longarm. His tone and manner were decidedly unfriendly. "Custis Long?" he asked around a wad of chewing tobacco.

"That's my name." Longarm said, noting the man's badge and the worn six-gun strapped low on his hip. Longarm stuck out his hand.

The marshal ignored the offered handshake. He was a big, heavyset man with muttonchop whiskers and a potbelly. He had deep-set eyes and a fist-busted nose. Longarm pegged him for a onetime rounder.

Spitting a long stream of tobacco juice onto the depot floor, the marshal barked, "Follow me."

Longarm bristled, taking an instant dislike to this man. People who knew Longarm quickly learned that a smile and a request would work wonders, but that a command would have quite the opposite reaction. "I'll be along soon enough."

"You'll come *now*!"

Longarm smiled, but there was no warmth in his expression when he drawled, "The hell you say."

The marshal had been about to turn and lead them out of the throng of milling train passengers, their friends, and their families when Longarm's words pulled him up short.

"Listen to me," the marshal said, swinging around and jabbing a finger at Longarm. "You may be someone out in Colorado. I don't know and I don't care. But this is Nevada and you're going to be working for me and taking my orders. And the first order is get your skinny ass moving and follow me!"

Longarm glanced over at Veronica Greenwald, who was standing nearby and gave him a nervous smile. Longarm had promised to wait and make sure that there was someone to greet Veronica from the new school where she was supposed to work. Unfortunately, it didn't look like anyone had bothered to welcome her to the West and serve as her escort.

"What's your name, Marshal?" Longarm said, turning his attention back to the big man.

"Denton. Bill Denton. Now—"

Longarm cut the man off short. "Well, Denton, you see this young schoolmarm waiting for someone to greet her?"

Denton scowled at Veronica. "Yeah. What about her?"

"I'm going to help her find the school where she is starting a new teaching job."

Denton exploded. "Don't you understand English? I said you're coming with me right now!"

Longarm gave up on the big fool. He turned on his heel toward Veronica, but Denton grabbed him by the shoulder and spun him around.

145

Longarm drove a powerful uppercut to Denton's protruding gut. The marshal was caught flat-footed with surprise. His mouth, twisted in anger, formed a big circle, and his eyes bugged as he sucked for air and tried to recover.

Longarm hit him again. And again. Denton weighed in at least fifty pounds heavier than Longarm, who was not about to give the marshal a chance to recover. The crowd parted like the Red Sea as Longarm drove Denton into a retreat across the depot floor. Each time the marshal tried to plant his feet and retaliate, Longarm's fist hammered his jaw or turned his big gut to jelly. Denton's nose cracked and flowed heavily. His lips were soon mashed to pulp, and one of his eyebrows was ripped by a slashing right uppercut. He was grunting with each blow, and when Longarm drew back and smashed him one final time, Denton flew off the baggage loading dock and landed on his back between two carriages waiting for hire.

"You all right, Marshal?" Longarm asked, flexing his fingers and then massaging his bruised knuckles as he gazed down at the man.

Denton *wasn't* all right. Longarm's blows had left his face a misshapen mass of welts and bruises. Furthermore, though his fall from the loading dock hadn't been a long one, only about four feet, the impact of his landing had emptied the last bit of oxygen from Denton's lungs. Bloodied, dazed, and unable to get his breath, Marshal Denton was a tragic sight as he lay between two spooked carriage horses who snorted and rolled their eyes in fear and suspicion.

"Tell you what," Longarm said. "I'll be along after I get Miss Greenwald settled. Okay?"

When Denton groaned, Longarm took that as a yes. "Okay," he said with a smile.

Longarm turned and walked back to the schoolteacher from Grover City, Iowa. "Doesn't look like anyone is going to be coming to meet you."

"No," Veronica said, trying to hide her disappointment. She pulled a letter from her purse and unfolded it. "This letter confirming my job was written by the principal of the Washoe School, a Mr. Arnold. He said to telegraph him when I'd arrive and he'd be sure that he was on hand to greet me."

"Well," Longarm said, sensing how badly the young woman felt, "maybe Mr. Arnold had a sudden emergency and couldn't get here on time. What's the address of the Washoe School?"

"It's on South Virginia Street."

"Heck," Longarm said with a smile, as he picked up his Winchester and baggage. "That'll be easy to find! Virginia is Reno's main street. Come along with me and I'll show you the town as we walk on down to meet your new employer."

Veronica brightened. "You are such a comfort! But did you really have to beat the living bee-jeezus out of that big, fat lawman?"

Longarm shrugged. "Well," he said, "I had a feeling that he was about to hit me so I needed to wallop him first. A rough fella like that will just knock you silly if he gets in the first good punch. So I wasn't taking any chances because he looked like a brawler. Truth of the matter is, I've had enough good whippings to last three lifetimes."

"You don't strike me as being the kind of man that anyone could whip, Custis."

"Well, that's not exactly true," he confessed as he led Veronica through the crowd and off toward Virginia Street. "One thing I learned at least ten years ago is that there are plenty of bigger and stronger men. When I was young, I didn't give a damn how big my opponent was, I'd wade in and stand toe to toe."

Longarm shook his head, remembering some of the awful poundings he'd taken when he was young and foolish enough to think that it was worth taking a beating in order to administer an even worse one.

"But you know, Veronica, after a few years and some broken bones and loose teeth, I learned my lesson. Now, I hit first and I hit hard. And if that doesn't work, I'm not averse to pistol-whipping some raging fool who needs a lesson in manners."

"I don't know how you are going to get back in good graces with that man."

"Maybe I won't," Longarm said, "but he won't likely be trying to boss me around anymore."

On the way down Virginia Street, Longarm explained how Reno had once been called Lake's Crossing, and had been a favorite resting place for the emigrant wagon trains that were about to struggle over the Sierras into the promise of a verdant California. The tragic Donner Party had made the mistake of resting their livestock too long, and then had suffered the consequences of their delay. Later, the builder of the Central Pacific Railroad, Charles Crocker, had renamed the town in honor of General Jesse Reno, a Union officer killed in 1862 by Indians. Since the discovery of the enormous bonanza on the Comstock, tons of gold and silver had been shipped down to Reno and sent both east and west on the railroad.

"This here is the Truckee River," Longarm said as they crossed the river that flowed through the town. "It spills out of Lake Tahoe, which is as pretty an alpine lake as there is in this country."

"I'd love to visit it someday."

"I'll take you the first chance we get," Longarm promised. "I swear that the water is as clear as your skin and as blue as your eyes. You can see rocks fifty feet under the surface."

"It sounds magnificent."

"It is." Longarm stopped for a moment on the bridge. He dropped his bags, leaned his big Winchester up against the bridge railing, then gently but firmly turned Veronica around and drew her close.

Her eyebrows lifted. "What are you doing?"

"I'm going to kiss you good-bye," Longarm said thumbing back his Stetson and grinning impishly. "You see, once we are at that school and we meet your new boss, I won't be able to do that without embarrassing you."

"You've got that figured right."

"So," Longarm said, "I'm kissing you now. Right here on the bridge in the middle of this town with all these folks watching. Veronica, I want this to be a kiss that you will never forget as long as you live."

"I already know that I won't forget it," she said, dropping her own bag and valise, then melting into his arms.

Longarm had kissed a lot of girls, but Veronica Greenwald was second to none. Her lips were soft and yielding, and her lilac-scented perfume made him giddy. He felt a great stir of passion in his loins, and it took all of his strength not to do something that might have embarrassed them both.

149

When they finally broke their kiss, Veronica was breathing as hard as if she'd run five miles up a mountainside, and Longarm was a little out of breath himself.

"My, my!" he said. "We should do that again!"

"Oh, no you don't!" Veronica cried, pulling away and grabbing up her bags. "If we do that again, I won't be able to think when I meet Mr. Arnold, much less talk about teaching."

Longarm laughed outright. "All right," he said, grabbing up his rifle and bags as they resumed walking down Virginia Street, "let's get back to business."

They chatted some more, but Longarm could sense that Veronica was greatly distracted. He would have liked to flatter himself by thinking it was his kiss, but more likely it was the sights and sounds of bustling Reno, and also the fact that Mr. Arnold had not thought enough of her to get to the train station.

"What's the address?"

"It's one hundred and five."

"Ought to be in the next block," Longarm announced. "After we get you introduced, we'll see about getting you settled into a respectable hotel or ladies' boardinghouse, and then I'd better hunt up Marshal Denton. If we don't shoot each other on sight, I guess we'll probably reach some kind of an understanding."

"We're both going to be very busy in the coming days," Veronica warned him. "I'm going to be the best teacher in this whole town. Every bit of my energy will be used to get started on the right foot."

"I'm sure you'll be a huge success."

"I mean to be," Veronica said with obvious determination. "It will take some getting used to living out in the

150

West, but I'm going to do everything I can to adjust. I've already fallen in love with those magnificent Sierra Nevada Mountains."

"They are beautiful," Longarm said, glancing up at the line of snowcapped peaks just a few miles to the west.

"And so, we may not have a chance to see each other very much for a while. I know all your energy will be directed toward catching that train gang."

"It sure will," Longarm agreed, "but when things settle down I'll come back to the school and look you up. We can go visit Lake Tahoe on a Sunday."

"It's a date," she said, "and . . ."

Longarm frowned, and his eyes followed Veronica's to the boarded-up Washoe School. It was a dilapidated wood-frame building with peeling paint and a broken-down picket fence. There was a note tacked to the door, and Longarm immediately sensed that the school was closed.

"I'd better read the note," Veronica said quietly as she stepped away from Longarm.

He felt awful, and wished there was something that he could do or say. But there wasn't, and so he just waited and watched the bags while Veronica went up and read the note.

She read it for a long time and when she finally returned, there were tears running down her cheeks. "It went broke," she told Longarm when she came to his side. "The note said that the bank repossessed Washoe School and all its property in default of unpaid mortgage payments."

"Damn," Longarm muttered.

Veronica gulped. "I don't even have enough money for a train ticket back to Iowa!"

"Calm down," Longarm said. "I can advance you the fare."

"But I don't want to go back to Iowa!"

"Then I can help you find a decent place to room until you can find another job."

"But what if I can't find one?"

"You will," Longarm assured her, though he had no idea what he was talking about. But Veronica looked so devastated that he added, "Why, a good schoolteacher is as prized in Nevada as squirrel eggs!"

"Squirrels don't lay eggs," she sniffled.

He used the cuff of his sleeve to dry her cheeks. "I know. That's why they're prized."

Veronica tried to laugh, but failed miserably. "Come on," Longarm said. "I know a lady who will take you into her home. She's a fine person and you'll be welcome until we can figure out exactly what you want to do."

"I'm worried about you losing your job. You should be doing something better than squiring me around."

"Mrs. Appleton lives just a few blocks away. She's a widow with a great and generous heart. You'll love her and she'll enjoy your company."

"You are *such* a sweet, dear man," Veronica said, kissing his cheek. "I don't know how I can ever repay your kindness."

"Oh, I imagine that I'll think of something," he said with a happy smile.

Betsy Appleton had been a madam for many years, but Longarm did not think he ought to mention that. She'd been very successful, saved some money, and invested a good deal more. She lived in a huge Victorian home on Fourth Street, not far from the Truckee River. It was a beautiful home, but Betsy had a soft spot for abandoned cats, dogs, and girls in just that order. The last time Longarm had visited Betsy, the old gal had had twenty-three cats and seven dogs, none of them housebroken.

"What's that smell?" Veronica asked as they mounted Betsy Appleton's huge veranda.

"Aw, she keeps a few cats and dogs inside."

This fact was vociferously confirmed a moment after Longarm knocked. All the dogs and cats set up a deafening chorus.

"I'm not sure about this," Veronica said with growing apprehension.

"You don't even notice the noise or smell after a few hours," Longarm assured her. "And Betsy sure could use some help feeding and cleaning up after them."

"Custis!"

Veronica would have turned and bolted away, except that Longarm grabbed and held her until Betsy opened her door.

"Custis!"

"Betsy, darlin'," he said, stepping up to give the sweet old gal a big hug and kiss on the cheek.

"And who is this lovely child?"

"Miss Veronica Greenwald, and she needs a little help right now, Betsy. Do you think she could stay until she finds a teaching job?"

Betsy was now in her sixties, but her skin was creamy smooth and her eyes were bright and trusting. "Why, of course! I'm sure that she'll love the children."

As they walked into the parlor, Betsy's "children" swarmed all around them. Big dogs. Little dogs. Pretty dogs. But mainly mangy dogs. Barking and yapping, with the cats in the background meowing. It was a real menagerie, and the odor of cat and dog droppings was almost overpowering.

"Of course she'll love your children, Betsy!" Longarm exclaimed, feeling light-headed in the closed room. "Why, Veronica was just telling me as we walked over here how much she loved animals."

"What a kind soul!" Betsy looked at Veronica. "What a dear heart you are. We shall become very good friends."

"I'm sure," Veronica said as a big, black dog began to lick her ankles, causing her to jump about like a carpet flea.

"Well, I have to run," Longarm hollered over the noise. "But I'll be back before you know it."

"Custis!"

Longarm could not bear to see Veronica's desperate expression, so he whirled and ran. He told himself that at least Veronica would be safe with Betsy Appleton, and might even be able to establish some control over the animals and housebreak them.

In any event, Veronica would have plenty of Betsy's "children" to teach.

Chapter 15

Longarm found Marshal Bill Denton's office, and checked to make sure that his gun was resting easy in its holster before he entered.

Denton wasn't in sight, but there was a young deputy on duty, and when he saw Longarm stroll through the door he paled.

"Hello there, young fella!" Longarm flashed his badge. "Deputy Marshal Custis Long from the Denver office. And what would your name be?"

The deputy, who had been reclining in an office chair, jumped to his feet, hand moving toward his six-gun.

"Whoa!" Longarm called, his own gun flashing up to draw a bead on the man. "Now what the hell is the matter with you? Haven't we got enough trouble with train robbers without trying to shoot each other?"

The deputy gulped. He was a tall, gangly fella with peach fuzz on his pimpled cheeks and a protruding Adam's apple that was bobbing up and down with fear. "Yes, sir!"

"Well, then, sit back down and let's get acquainted,"

Longarm said, returning his six-gun to its holster and resting his Winchester against a wall. "Where is Marshal Denton?"

"He's in the hospital, Mr. Long! You beat the shit of him and when he fell off that loading dock, he screwed up his back."

"Damn," Longarm said, "I am genuinely sorry about that. I hope he isn't froze up or anything."

"No, he's not froze but he's in some pain. Doctor says you also broke his nose and cracked his jaw. He's going to be out of commission for a couple of months."

"Damn," Longarm repeated. "I didn't realize that he'd taken that fight so hard."

"What fight? From what I hear, he never got in a punch. And believe me, no one has ever whipped Marshal Denton in a fair fight."

"There isn't such a thing as a 'fair fight,'" Longarm said. "I'll bet you that Marshal Denton has pistol-whipped plenty of men or dropped them with a single punch."

"Yeah, sure! But he's the marshal!"

"He was in serious need of a lesson in manners," Longarm said. "You see, we're all in this together. And unless a man who wears the badge proves himself incompetent or corrupt, there's an unspoken rule that we treat each other with courtesy and respect. Your marshal broke that rule, and when he laid his hand on me, I had little choice but to teach him a hard, hard lesson."

"Well, he's going to kill you when he can get up and walk."

Longarm clucked his tongue. "I don't know how men like Denton ever last in government service. And as for 'killing me,' well, I'll just face that if and when it happens."

"It'll happen."

"Maybe." Longarm sat down heavily. "I always thought that a man should not worry too much about the future. Most of our fears never materialize. Those that do aren't ever as bad as we expect them to be."

Longarm smiled disarmingly. "Now, what is your name?"

"Deputy Ronald Dudley."

"Glad to meet you, Ron. We have our work cut out for us on this railroad case. Have you been up to Donner Pass to see the damage?"

"No. The marshal told me that he was going to go up there with you, but . . . well, he won't be even getting out of the hospital bed for a while."

"The man should have been up there hours after the wreck, looking for clues or leads."

"Reno is a pretty wild town, Mr. Long."

"Custis. You call me Custis."

"Yes, sir. Well, Custis, there are just the two of us and this is a tough town."

"No tougher than Rock Springs or Cheyenne and they only have one lawman." Longarm frowned. "Ron, we need to get up to Donner Pass first thing. When does the next train leave?"

"In about fifteen minutes. It's the same one that you rode in on. It's still got to get over the hump before it ends its run in Sacramento."

Longarm was hungry and tired, but he knew that he could not afford to delay this trip for even a day. "Grab your coat and let's go, Ron."

157

"I can't leave here now! There's no one else to keep a lid on this town! Why, what if someone robbed the bank? Or there was a murder?"

"If it happens, it happens and we'll just have to take care of it when we return."

"Dammit! I just can't go!"

Longarm could see that the young man was determined to remain at his desk no matter what. "All right," he said, "I'll go on up myself and see if there is anything left worth noting. Have you had any snow or rain since the derailment?"

"One storm came through and dropped a few inches of snow."

"Well, then, I'm probably wasting my time even going up there, but I'd better do it anyway. I'll leave my bags here since I haven't had time to check into a room."

"They'll be safe."

"I wonder," Longarm said, making it clear that he was not the least bit impressed with the deputy.

As he started out the door on his way back to the train, Ron called out, "There's a railroad official handling the investigation from their side of things. He is definitely the man you want to talk to!"

Longarm stopped in the doorway and turned. "What's his name and where can I find him?"

"His name is Bruce Pettibone. I never even met the man, but I'm told he can be found at Donner Pass or else at the railroad's western headquarters in Sacramento."

"Thanks," Longarm said.

"Will you report what you found?" Ron smiled weakly. "Marshal Denton is going to want to know what you're up to."

"Why? So he can back-shoot me when he's able to crawl out of his hospital bed?"

"He's a better man than that," Ron said defensively. "You two just got off on the wrong foot."

"No," Longarm corrected, "I offered him my hand in friendship and cooperation and he looked at me like some kind of bug. He didn't *ask* me to come with him, he ordered me. Men like your boss never seem to learn that you get along better in life when you treat people as equals. Wouldn't you agree, Deputy Dudley?"

Ron blushed and dipped his pointy chin.

"I'll report back," Longarm said. "And if there is a bank robbery or murder, you've only to ask and I'll assist you in any way that I can."

"Thank you very much," Dudley said with an embarrassed grin. "I ain't been on this job more than a few weeks. I don't even know if I'm cut out for it, but I just got married and I needed work. My wife is scared to death that I'm going to get beat up or shot."

"It goes with the territory," Longarm said. "My advice to you is to treat people with respect and not follow Denton's bad example. He might be big and strong enough to bully people, but you aren't."

"I know that, sir."

Longarm paused. "I can't advise you on what to do, but I will say this. The old adage says that it is not the size of the dog but the size of the dog's fight that counts. I've known some deputies that didn't weigh much more than a hundred pounds soaking wet, and they commanded all the authority and respect they needed or ever wanted. And I've known big, tough men like Denton who bullied men and then got waylaid or ambushed and sent to Boot Hill."

Longarm heard the sound of the train whistle announcing its imminent departure. "Ron, you go ahead and talk softly, but learn how to use both a gun and a rifle better than any man in this town. If you do that, and people see that you're serious about your job, they'll treat you right and there won't be a problem that you cannot handle."

"Yes, sir!"

Longarm barely made it to the train. It was slowly rolling west toward the steep Sierra foothills when Longarm swung on board the caboose. Gasping and wheezing in the cold, thin air, he staggered into the mail car and collapsed on a bench with the heavy Winchester still clenched in his hand.

A railroad signalman with ruddy cheeks and an Irish smile said, "Welcome back aboard, Marshal Long! Thought you'd left us for good. Glad to see you again."

"Thanks. You wouldn't happen to have a little whiskey hidden about somewhere, would you?"

"Are there shamrocks in Ireland?"

Longarm laughed. "I do believe there are."

"Then," the man said with a twinkle in his eyes, "there is *Irish* whiskey to be found in this car!"

There was actually quite a bit of Irish whiskey stuffed into hidden places on board. And as the train struggled mightily up a steep grade built along the rushing Truckee River, Longarm and signalman Liam O'Neil enjoyed it to the fullest.

"How far are you goin'?" Liam asked as he passed the bottle to Longarm.

"To the wreck at Donner Pass."

"Oh," Liam said, with a solemn shake of his head. "Now that was an awful thing! A terrible thing!"

"I was on the train that was blown off the tracks at Laramie Summit," Longarm said. "So I know how bad it is."

"Oh, I hope you catch 'em! It would be a fine day for this railroad and we'd celebrate."

"I'll catch them," Longarm vowed, looking out the window at the rugged mountains that they were trying to crest.

He thought of the gang member he'd shot at the Laramie blacksmith shop, of Blake Huntington's dead and glass-cut body lying in an alley behind the Outpost Hotel, of the fella he'd killed in the shootout at the ranch house, and finally of Fergus in the mail car.

"Liam, I take no satisfaction in saying this, but I've already killed four men that were part of that train-robbing bunch. I'll never know exactly what role each played, but they were all somehow connected."

"And were they also a part of the gang that did the evil work at Donner Pass?"

"I think so." Longarm took a pull on the bottle of Irish whiskey. "Do you live in Reno?"

"I do!"

"Then do you know the name of an important state senator that made a fortune on the Comstock Lode, but then lost it again on mining stocks?"

"That sounds like Senator George Howard. He's up for reelection and it's almost sure that we'll vote the bastard out of office."

"He's incompetent?"

"He's a crook!" Liam's voice turned hard. "He's got

161

his hands into every dirty game in western Nevada. More is the wonder that he hasn't been hanged by the vigilantes before now."

"Where does he live?"

"In Reno. Somewhere over in the fancy part of town." Liam raised his eyebrows. "And why would you be askin'?"

"I've got my reasons."

"Is he in cahoots with this gang?"

"I didn't say that."

"You didn't need to, Marshal. I can see the hunter's lust gleaming in your eyes. You're like an Irish setter hunting pheasants in the field. You've the nose for blood and the heart for the hunt."

Longarm shrugged and took another drink. "What do you know about this fella named Bruce Pettibone?"

"Oh," Liam said, eyebrows lifting, "there's a good man!"

Longarm was surprised. It was his experience that most railroad detectives and administrators were long on corporate politics and short on good sense. "For a fact?"

"Sure! Mr. Pettibone is a fine man and a brave one too! He's tracked down and shot outlaws who tried to rob the Union Pacific. He has!"

"Well," Longarm said, "in that case, I'm looking forward to meeting Mr. Bruce Pettibone."

Chapter 16

The trip up to Donner Lake was slow but picturesque. The lower, sage-covered hills gave way to Douglas fir and ponderosa pine and the air became even colder. From the sheltered comfort of a coach, Longarm watched freighters using oxen, mules, and horses as they struggled up the winding and muddy road toward Lake Tahoe.

The train passed through immense wooden snowsheds that jutted out from the mountainside to shunt off avalanches and keep the tracks open after the worst of the winter storms. A good thousand feet below Donner Summit snow blanketed the ground, and Longarm knew that it was going to be almost impossible to find any evidence around the wreck of the train. He knew that most of whatever new information he would learn would have to come from Bruce Pettibone.

The train passed above Donner Lake, frozen and glazed with fresh snow. When they arrived at the depot, Longarm was the only passenger to disembark. The train did take on two freezing passengers, and then waited to load some cargo before pulling out of the depot for Sacramento.

"Good luck to you!" Liam shouted. "You catch and

hang them bloody train-wreckin' bastards!"

"I'll do my best," Longarm called, watching as Liam went to help another train employee load some heavy wooden crates into the mail car.

The train depot at Donner Pass wasn't much. In the summertime, there was a heavy influx of people seeking the cool relief of the mountains. There were a few log cabins nearby, but most of those were down near the lake. Longarm entered the depot and headed for the ticket cage.

"Good afternoon," he said. "I'm looking for Mr. Bruce Pettibone. Is he around?"

"Yep. But you'd better hurry outside because he's about to board that train for Sacramento."

"He can't do that!"

The ticket man shrugged. "There are very few men that can tell Mr. Pettibone what to do. But it's a free country and you're welcome to try. You can see him through that window. Short, handsome fella in the red woolen mackinaw."

Pettibone was a round bundle of energy and motion. Barely five and a half feet tall, he was uncommonly wide-shouldered. Longarm's first impression was of a beer barrel with arms and legs. He was baby-faced, but obviously not young because his hair was shot with silver.

"Mr. Pettibone!" Longarm called, hurrying after the man.

Pettibone turned. "Yes?"

Longarm fumbled for his badge. "I'm a federal deputy marshal from Denver and I believe that the Laramie Summit derailment was committed by the same people that also derailed the train at Donner Pass."

"What makes you think so?"

"It's a long story."

"I'm sorry, Deputy, but I've got to return to Sacramento."

The man started to walk past, but Longarm blocked his path. "I need your help. The people who wrecked your train are the same ones that sent the train I was riding in over the edge of a mountain just east of Laramie Summit."

"My investigation tells me that is entirely possible. However, I'm working alone on this case."

"Do you have any suspects?"

"No, not really, but—"

"I've killed four of the men that belong to the same gang that you are hunting." Longarm looked Pettibone square in the eyes. "And I have names."

Pettibone blinked. "You have names?"

"That's right."

Pettibone glanced at the men as they finished loading the crates. The train blasted its steam whistle, and he and Longarm could hear the couplings strain as the big drivers that had pulled the train up the mountain began to roll forward.

"Give them to me!"

But Longarm shook his head. "I'll be damned if I'm going to help you or your railroad if you won't cooperate in this investigation."

Pettibone's face darkened with anger. The train began to move slowly. "If you have suspects, I can work from Sacramento while you operate out of Reno. We can use the telegraph and probably be more effective than if we worked together."

"We work together here or not at all," Longarm said bluntly. "And unless your career depends on you getting on board that train, I suggest you miss it and take me out to the wreck. I want to see it and hear everything that you know."

"Is that right?" Pettibone exclaimed with exasperation. "Well, when in tarnation would I get to hear the names of your supposed suspects?"

"Right afterward."

Pettibone was a man torn between exasperation, curiosity, and desire. Very likely he considered that Longarm could not deliver the promised goods or that the names he had were worthless. Very likely he also had someone waiting at the Sacramento depot for him who would be very disappointed if he did not show up.

"Give me just one of your suspects' names!"

Longarm balanced his Winchester across his chest. "All right," he agreed, "let's start at the top of the dung heap. The mastermind who planned and probably financed the derailment of both trains is no less than State Senator George Howard."

Pettibone gaped with astonishment. He seemed to have trouble finding words. Finally he stammered, "It's taken me thousands of hours of investigation to reach that same conclusion! How did you—"

"Your Sacramento train is leaving," Longarm said. "The question I have is, are you going or are you staying with me until we break this case?"

Pettibone took a deep breath. "I'm staying," he decided. "Let's go back inside where we can talk in my office."

On the way in, Pettibone called to the ticket man to locate the depot's telegraph operator. "Tell him to wire

166

the Sacramento depot where my wife and two sons will be expecting me in about three hours. Tell him to say that I have been delayed and will come home as soon as possible."

"Yes, sir!"

"This way," Pettibone growled as he rolled across the depot lobby and used a key to unlock an unmarked door.

Pettibone's office was in a clutter, which was a credit to the man as far as Longarm was concerned. Show Longarm a neat lawman or detective and he'd show you a man that did not have enough to do.

"Sit down," Pettibone ordered.

"No," Longarm said, dropping his bags and leaning his Winchester up against a scarred file case. "I want to inspect the site of the derailment and then hear what you know before I tell you anymore."

"I'm in charge here!"

Longarm shook his head. "You know, that's exactly the same attitude that got Marshal Denton all banged up and admitted to the hospital."

"Denton is in the hospital?"

"Yep." Longarm massaged his bruised and skinned knuckles, and the meaning was very clear.

Pettibone's scowl melted and he even grinned. "Well, I'll be damned! I thought that I was the one that was finally going to have to take that big bastard down a peg or two."

Longarm said nothing.

"Listen," Pettibone continued, "any man that can whip Denton is a man that I can respect. Do you have any proof about Senator Howard?"

"Not yet."

Pettibone frowned. "All right," he said. "Have you ever worn snowshoes?"

"Once."

"Good! We'll strap on a couple pairs and go for a walk in the woods. It's just up the tracks about a mile, but you won't be able to reach the wrecked cars. They tumbled far down in a frozen gorge."

"That's what also happened at Laramie Summit," Longarm said. "These boys that are derailing the trains aren't delicate or fair-minded, are they?"

"No," Pettibone said, "they damn sure aren't."

It took the better part of an hour to reach the site of the train wreck, and there really wasn't a lot to see once they arrived, but then Longarm did not need to see much.

"The method of derailment is the same," Longarm announced. "They dynamited the track just as the locomotive passed over it."

"Not dynamite," Pettibone corrected. "They used nitroglycerine."

"What?"

"It's banned because of its instability and power. The Central Pacific had to resort to its use when they were building the Sierra summit tunnels. Nitroglycerine has so much power that it once leveled an entire city block over in San Francisco. The stuff is extremely unstable but very, very powerful. It would take several cases of dynamite to lift a locomotive off the tracks, but just a jar of liquid nitroglycerine."

"All right," Longarm said, "I'll go along with that. But so what?"

"I've been checking on every chemist in California and Nevada. One of them has to be mixing and handling that stuff. I'm expecting a telegram any day that will link Senator Howard to a criminal who also happens to be a skilled chemist."

"Why don't we just keep an eye on the senator?"

"Because he is too smart to ever get personally involved in this. He'll use intermediaries. The only way we nail him is to catch someone who deals with him and is willing to testify against the senator in court."

"So where do you suggest we start?"

"We start with your list of names. Are you ready to give them to me now?"

Longarm supposed he was. One by one, he reeled off the names that Fergus had given him, and as he did so, Pettibone's grin widened.

"You like what you've heard?"

"Damn right I do! Big Tom Canyon, Two-Fingered Earl, Shorty Hamilton, and most all the others are living in a cabin not twenty miles from here. They're at the north shore of Lake Tahoe."

It was Longarm's turn to grin. "You don't say!"

"I do say. But we'll never get them arrested without evidence."

Longarm patted his six-gun. "Evidence is usually found at the source. I'm going to that cabin and find it."

"Whoa!" Pettibone cried. "You can't just . . ."

"Just what?"

"Go busting in there!"

"Watch me," Longarm said.

Pettibone was better on snowshoes than Longarm and managed to get in front of him. "You don't even know which cabin they're at."

"I'll find it. You said it's the north shore of Lake Tahoe.

Now kindly step out of my path."

Pettibone shook his head. "Tell me, Deputy Long, have you always been so headstrong and impetuous?"

"I'm not one for planning and jawin' a whole hell of a lot, if that's what you mean."

"That's exactly what I mean."

"Are you coming or not?"

"I'm coming," Pettibone said, "though I'm half afraid that you're bound to make my wife a widow."

"You can stay if you want," Longarm told the man. "I'll not hold it against you."

"That's mighty kind, but I wouldn't miss this roundup for anything."

"How can we get there the quickest?"

"By not taking off these snowshoes."

Longarm nodded. "I've got a rifle back at your depot and if you have a shotgun or something, that might help."

"I do have one."

"Are you any good in a gunfight?"

Pettibone expelled a deep, frosty breath. "I honestly do not know. I'm pretty good with my fists."

"You'll do," Longarm decided, working on intuition and professional judgment. "Now let's find that cabin!"

170

Chapter 17

Longarm had never spent such a miserable afternoon as he did that day trying to keep up with Bruce Pettibone on snowshoes. The railroad detective was inexhaustible, and seemed intent on driving Longarm until he dropped. Fortunately, the air was crisp and the trail already broken and mostly leading downhill. They skirted Bald and Lookout Mountains to the southwest and crossed any number of frozen creeks as they hurried through the heavy pine forests.

When the sun began to slide behind the mountains and Longarm still could not see Lake Tahoe, he shouted, "Hold up there, dammit!"

"What's wrong?" Pettibone asked, his breath coming in short, frosty bursts.

"What's wrong is that you're about to kill me!"

"But this is all downhill!"

"Uphill or downhill, I'm bushed!" Longarm adjusted his Winchester, which he had rigged on a sling and thrown over his shoulder. "I don't figure I want to go much farther today. Pettibone, what do you say we make a camp and get an early start in the morning?"

"You mean sleep in this damned snow?" Pettibone looked appalled.

"We can make a dry camp if we start preparing it before dark. Maybe cut some pine boughs and—"

"Listen," Pettibone said. "Storms up here come fast and frequent in the winter. Now, even if I had enough blankets—which I don't—I wouldn't even consider spending the night out here."

"Then what can we consider, being as how I'm about to collapse from fatigue?"

Pettibone looked up at the dying sun. "I say we have just another three miles to the lake. Their cabin is at Agate Bay and we could be there soon after dark."

"Yeah, but what is the damned hurry?"

Pettibone looked disgusted. "It's just that, since you decided we should do this, I'd like to get it done."

"There's no sense in charging into all those men half-cocked," Longarm said. "In any case, I'm too damned cold and tired to be any good in a fight."

Pettibone swore under his breath. "All right," he finally said. "A friend of mine has a summer cabin just up ahead. We can stay there for the night and leave early in the morning."

"Fine."

Longarm followed the railroad man on down the hill, and they struggled on for about another half hour before they came to the cabin. It wasn't much, and Pettibone had to break a window to get inside. But there was some food and blankets and even chopped firewood.

Much later, fed and warmed by the fire, Longarm smoked a cheroot and said, "I rode with a nice fella up from Reno in the train's mail car."

"That'd be Liam. Did he offer you a drink of that Irish whiskey?"

"He did," Longarm said.

"Then that's why you ran out of steam. Strong spirits rob a man of his vitality, you know."

"Are you a Mormon?"

"No, but I am a teetotaler. I swore off the stuff when I saw what it did to my father. It turned him into a raving maniac. He finally shot himself when I was about sixteen."

"I'm sorry to hear that."

"Don't be. It was the best thing he could have done for the family. It also taught me never to forget how fast liquor can ruin a good man."

"Do you smoke?" Longarm patted his coat pocket. "I've got a couple more cigars."

"Nope."

Longarm shook his head. "Pettibone, if you don't drink and you don't smoke, then you might as well be a Mormon."

"Listen to you," Pettibone said with amusement. "Why, you were gasping like a locomotive out there on the trail! It's that tobacco that robs your wind and ruins your lungs."

"A man has got to have a few pleasures in life."

Pettibone studied Longarm in the firelight. "I'll bet you have pleasures aplenty with the ladies, isn't that so?"

"I like 'em fine," Longarm replied. "But someday I might settle down and have a family. Like you."

"I don't think so."

Longarm curbed his annoyance. He didn't understand

173

how this man could make such an important assessment, given that they were almost strangers.

"I was a sheriff once," Pettibone said after several minutes of strained silence.

"For a fact?"

"Yes. It was on the Comstock Lode. I was, for a few short and exciting months, the sheriff at Gold Hill."

"Sure, I've been through there dozens of times. Why'd you quit?"

"I killed an innocent man," Pettibone said quietly. "His only crime was that he was drunk."

"Did he go for his gun?"

"A knife. I thought he was passed out and when I reached down to drag him into a chair, he probably thought I was about to steal what little money he had left in his pockets. So he yanked out his knife and stabbed me in the side."

"Then he wasn't innocent if he used a knife against you, Pettibone."

"Oh, yes he was! You see, he didn't know what he was doing. And instead of kicking his boots to wake him up first so that sort of thing didn't happen, I just grabbed him. To make matters worse, when he stabbed me, I instinctively slammed the heel of my hand up into his nose."

Pettibone shook his head, his expression bleak. "It was pure reaction. There were dozens of witnesses and they all said that I was just trying to push him away, not drive nasal bones into the drunken man's brain."

Longarm smoked in silence. He could see how troubled Pettibone was over this unfortunate death, and felt sure that everyone had already said all the consoling words but none of them had counted. In Bruce Pettibone's mind, he was guilty of murder. Not a vicious or premeditated murder, but a murder caused by ignorance.

Pettibone looked up suddenly. "You've killed a lot of men, haven't you?"

It wasn't a question and Longarm didn't reply.

"Doesn't it bother you?"

"Sometimes." Longarm blew a smoke ring at the fire. He could hear the wind through the pines outside and he was very grateful that they weren't camped in the freezing snow.

"Will it bother you tomorrow if we have to kill those train robbers?"

"Not a whit," Longarm growled. "You saw the results of what they did to the train at this end. Well, it was about as bad at Laramie Summit. They killed women and old men. They didn't even know who they killed, and they didn't care that some of them lived for a while in the freezing cold and died in pain."

Longarm looked hard at Bruce Pettibone. "Listen to me," he said, his voice taking on an edge. "If you haven't the stomach for the fight, then you should return to the depot in the morning. I don't need a good family man who hesitates and gets himself killed for nothing."

"Maybe we can get the drop on the whole bunch and take them without firing a single shot."

"Not very damned likely," Longarm said. "The odds are that we will have a gunfight. The odds are that unless we drop two or three in the first volley, we won't live to see spring. So you need to decide if you are ready to fight or not."

After a long few minutes, Pettibone said, "I'll fight if they don't surrender."

"You just have that shotgun cocked and ready. In your mind, figure to unload both barrels. Otherwise, you're a dead man. Mark my words, Pettibone. The outlaws we are going to brace are tough, and they sure won't be willing to surrender so they can march to a gallows."

Pettibone nodded. "I guess that's probably the best way to look at it."

"It's the *only* way to look at it," Longarm told him.

Longarm fed the fire until it was hot, and then lay back on his blankets and drifted off to sleep wondering if he or Pettibone would survive the next day.

"Wake up," Pettibone said, jostling Longarm.

Longarm sat up out of a dead sleep and looked around. For a moment he forgot where he was, but then he spotted Pettibone. He could see that the railroad detective had rustled up and cooked some breakfast. Biscuits, salt pork, and mercy, even coffee.

"I ought to bring you along on these manhunts more often," Longarm said when he was served a heaping breakfast plate.

"Well, you complained so bad last evening about being weak and exhausted that I figured I'd better try and get your strength back if we're to have any chance of surviving the day."

Longarm glanced up from his plate. "You know, you can still back out. Just give me the loan of your shotgun and go on back to Donner Pass."

"Oh, no!" Pettibone said. "Besides, you've already got a six-gun on your hip and a Model '73 Winchester. I imagine that you're also packing some kind of hideout gun. So I just don't see that you need any more weapons. What you need is more hands, and mine will have to do."

"They'll do fine," Longarm said with a smile.

When they finished breakfast and packed their gear, they laced on the snowshoes and headed on down the trail. In less than an hour they saw the lake, shimmering like an emerald in the early morning sun.

"It's beautiful," Pettibone said. "I swear it's the prettiest sight that I've ever laid eyes upon—except for my wife."

"Of course." Longarm shielded his eyes against the rising sun. "Where is Agate Bay and the cabin?"

"Straight ahead." Pettibone replied.

Longarm followed the man on down into the volcanic basin that cupped Lake Tahoe. It was still very early and, if they were in luck, it was even possible that they could yet catch the gang asleep. Such men lived hard, and would stay up half the night drinking, playing cards, and whoring, and sleep late the next day.

Longarm hoped that was the case now. Otherwise, things were going to become very exciting indeed in the next hour.

Chapter 18

It was too fine a morning to die. Much too fine, Longarm decided as he advanced silently toward the cabin. He and Pettibone had already circled the hideout and discovered the outlaws' horses corralled back in the trees. Now it was just a matter of getting the drop on this bunch before they had time to wake up and mount any form of resistance.

Pettibone was advancing on the cabin from the opposite side, and it was decided that Longarm would be the first one through the door, going low, while the railroad detective would come in standing up with his double-barreled shotgun ready to roar.

Longarm's heart was pounding as he stepped up to the cabin and placed his hand on the doorknob. He listened for any sign that the gang was awake, but heard nothing but snoring.

"Are you ready?" he whispered to Pettibone.

Pettibone gripped the shotgun in his fists and nodded.

Longarm turned the knob in his left hand, and when it was open a crack, he hefted his Winchester in his left hand while his right hand clenched his six-gun. Very slowly, he eased the door open, took a quick step inside, and dropped to one knee.

"Everyone freeze!" he bellowed. "You're under arrest!"

It was dim in the cabin. Too dim to see anything but shadows and silhouettes. But not too dim to detect movement. The outlaws all went for their guns. The entire room exploded with panic and gunfire. Longarm felt a bullet graze his neck and he flattened, gun belching bullets and fire. Behind him he heard Pettibone grunt, and knew the man was hit even as the shotgun boomed twice. Pettibone tumbled back outside, and the hammer of Longarm's gun struck an empty. He dropped the weapon, dragged his Winchester up, and began to pound heavy lead into the darkness.

In moments, the interior of the cabin was filled with gunsmoke and the wails of wounded and dying men. When the return fire died, Longarm scrambled back out the door and hurried to Pettibone's side. The railroad detective had been hit by a bullet across his temple which had also ripped away the top half of his right ear. Pettibone was bleeding, but more dazed than anything.

"Don't let all that blood buffalo you," Longarm said. "You're going to live to earn a railroad citation for bravery. Reload that shotgun because we might not be finished."

Even as Longarm was speaking, Eli Wheat crashed through the cabin's lone front window. He rolled in the snow, then jumped up and sprinted toward the trees.

"Stop!" Longarm shouted, dragging his Winchester to his shoulder. "Damn you, Eli, freeze!"

But Eli didn't freeze. He spun around and fired back at Longarm, narrowly missing, probably because snow or even blood was fouling his vision. Cursing, Eli whirled and vanished into the forest running hard. Longarm had no chance to drop the killer before he disappeared.

"Listen to me, Pettibone!" Longarm yelled. "If there's anyone left alive in this cabin with a mind to escape, you've got to drop them with that shotgun. Do you understand me?"

"Yeah," Pettibone said, lowering a bloody hand from where the top of his ear had been.

When the railroad man began to reload, Longarm knew that Pettibone was going to be able to guard the cabin door and take care of himself.

"I'll be right back," he vowed before he whirled and raced after Eli.

Eli was fast and he was desperate. Wherever he crossed patches of snow, Eli left a crimson stain. Longarm knew that the man would never be taken alive. His tracks angled to the lake's shoreline. In some places, the shore was soft with mud and Eli had sunk deep but kept running. Just ahead there was a small peninsula where the pines crowded the edge of the water. When Longarm was within fifty yards of that place, Eli jumped out of the trees and opened fire.

Longarm felt a bullet whine past his face. He dove into the moss and muck alongside the lake and tried to bring his rifle to bear on Eli, but the man was gone again.

"Damn!" Longarm shouted, jumping up covered with mud and half-frozen muck. He slogged onward knowing that he made a great target.

It was not until Longarm had crossed the peninsula and broken back into the open that he saw the fugitive had commandeered a rowboat and was madly rowing across the big lake. Tahoe, unlike the much smaller and shallower Donner Lake, had not frozen, although it was rimmed by shore ice. Longarm searched in vain for another boat, and when he saw that Eli would escape, dropped to one knee and took aim at the rowboat's hull.

"Eli!" he shouted. "Turn around and row back!"

Longarm's voice carried strongly across the freezing, choppy water. "You hear me!" he yelled. "This is Deputy Custis Long and you're not getting away from me again! Now stop and row back!"

"Go to hell!" Eli screamed, oars flashing in the morning sun.

Longarm could have shot Eli, but he wanted him alive. The man was still less than three hundred yards out, but he was pulling away fast. Longarm had no choice. He fired, and saw the hull of the wooden rowboat splinter at the water line.

"Aim lower!" he muttered to himself.

His next bullet struck the waterline, ricocheted like a flat rock, and then exploded through the wooden hull. Longarm heard Eli scream as much in fury as in fear. Eli yanked off his jacket and desperately tried to plug the hole.

Longarm began to methodically riddle the rowboat. Each bullet ripped through the hull right at the waterline. He was careful not to hit Eli because he was sure that the killer would leap into the water and swim back resigned to face that Denver hangman.

But Eli fooled him. The man just kept rowing even as his boat took on more water and began to sink.

"You can't make it!" Longarm yelled. "Jump and swim back!"

"Go to hell!" Eli screamed. "I can't swim!"

Longarm lowered his rifle and came to his feet. He stood rooted to the muddy shore as Eli spun the oars and the rowboat slowly sank. Longarm felt sure that the outlaw would leap into the water and attempt to cling to the wooden hull, and maybe that was Eli's intention. But the rowboat was old and water-logged, so the thing just sank.

"Help! Help me, Deputy Long!" Eli screamed, hanging onto an oar and trying to make it support his weight. The oar, however, was too light.

The corners of Longarm's mouth twisted down as he watched the drowning. Eli Wheat fought the freezing water for several minutes, and then he disappeared in a swirl of bubbles.

When Longarm returned to the cabin, he found Bruce Pettibone inside, attending to the wounded and the dying.

"How many are going to make it?"

"Big Tom Canyon is dead. Hawk Jenkins is too. Two-Fingered Earl is lung-shot and he just drowned in his own blood. Indian Red Lopez won't last through the next hour."

"Who does that leave?"

"Hamilton and Orr. Both are wounded but they're going to live."

"Good. We'll need confessions and evidence against Senator Howard."

"I've already gotten it. They're so spooked that I didn't even have to ask about the senator. They volunteered the information."

"How are you doing?"

"I thought I was a goner," Pettibone admitted. "I saw my entire life flash before my eyes."

"For a fact?"

"No," Pettibone said, "but it sounded good. I'll be fine. Maybe I'll look a little funny with just half a right ear, but I'm not complaining."

"And neither will your wife and children," Longarm said.

"What happened to the one that came out through he window and you chased after?"

"He drowned in the lake."

"Drowned?"

"That's right. If they manage to fish out his body, they won't find any bullet holes. At least none that proved fatal."

Pettibone looked around at the slaughterhouse filled with dead and dying men. He shook his head. "I won't ever forget what happened here."

"Me neither," Longarm said, stepping out of the cabin and dragging in some clean, cold air.

The next day there wasn't much else that people in northern Nevada talked or read about other than how Longarm and Bruce Pettibone had survived a terrible gun battle with the notorious train-robbing gang at Lake Tahoe, and how the only two surviving outlaws would turn state's evidence against Senator Howard in exchange for their lives.

Longarm had sent a telegram to Billy Vail telling his boss that the reign of terror against the Union Pacific and its innocent passengers was over. Billy's answering telegram had come back within the hour.

NICE WORK STOP NED ROWE CAUGHT IN CHEYENNE BY FEDERAL AGENTS STOP RETURN

TO DENVER FOR CELEBRATION STOP GLAD TO HEAR THAT TAHOE FISHES WILL EAT WHEAT STOP

The last line of the telegraph gave Longarm a belly laugh. The first he'd enjoyed in a good long while. He briefly considered visiting Veronica Greenwald, but changed his mind. Betsy would take care of Veronica, who'd probably be married or teaching kids the next time that Longarm passed through Reno.

Besides, Longarm thought as he boarded the eastbound transcontinental, he wanted to stay a few days in Laramie with Milly, and then another couple days in Cheyenne to make sure that Wyoming's newest lady attorney was off to a successful start.

By then, Billy would be fit to be tied and have canceled the celebration. That would be a shame, but Longarm figured that a man could only spread himself around just so much.

Watch for

LONGARM ON THE FEVER COAST

183rd novel in the bold LONGARM series
from Jove

Coming in March!